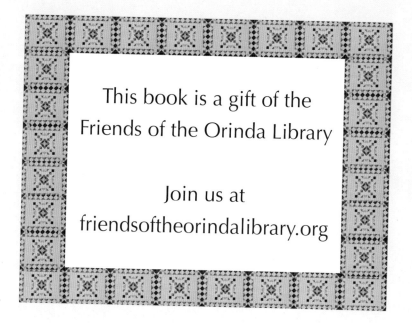

MARINA MANDER

the first true lie

WITHDRAWN

HOGARTH
NEW YORK

Published in the United States by Hogarth, an imprint of the Crown
Publishing Group, a division of Random House LLC, a Penguin Random
House Company, New York.

www.crownpublishing.com

HOGARTH is a trademark of the Random House Group Limited, and the H
colophon is a trademark of Random House LLC.

Originally published in Italy as *La prima vera bugia* by et al. edizioni, Milan,
in 2011.
Copyright © 2011 by et al. S.r.l.
Copyright © 2011 by Marina Mander.

Library of Congress Cataloging-in-Publication Data
Mander, Marina, 1963-
  [Prima vera bugia. English]
 The first true lie : a novel / Marina Mander.
    pages cm
  Translation of: La prima vera bugia. 1a ed. Milano : Et al., 2011.
1. Boys—Fiction. 2. Mothers and sons—Fiction. 3. Mothers—Death—
Fiction. 4. Self-actualization (Psychology)—Fiction. 5. Identity
(Psychology)—Fiction. 6. Psychological fiction. I. Title.
  PQ4873.A4734P7513 2014
  853'.914—dc23

                    2013027740

ISBN 978-0-770-43685-8
eBook ISBN 978-0-770-43686-5

Printed in the United States of America

Book design by Elina D. Nudelman
Cover design by Elena Giavaldi
Cover photographs: Donald Iain Smith/Flickr/Getty

10 9 8 7 6 5 4 3 2 1

First Edition

the first true lie

Some Days

Some days I wonder: What does it mean to be a half orphan?

You can't know, because you're a grown-up.

You've got parents who already seem like grand-parents, a house where you're free to go into all the rooms, a car to get away in…There are so many things you can forget.

Mama's always saying "I remember," but I'm not so sure about that because sometimes it seems she really doesn't remember anything about what it's like to be my age. This happens a lot with adults.

The worst are the ones who take your toys and then don't even know how to play. They want to win, but they can't handle losing, and as soon as you start to have fun, they suddenly remember they've got an appointment, or they've parked the car badly, or else it's their kid.

"Sorry, love, but I really must be off now."

The worst are the ones who ignore you and shut them-selves up in the bedroom with Mama.

"We're going to go in there for a bit to chat."

They say they have to talk, but I know perfectly well they're having sex. They turn the lock so, so slowly and hardly talk at all and every once in a while Mama yelps and then goes *Shhhh*.

Mama thinks I never notice anything because her room is at the end of the hall, but I've realized that if I want to protect myself I can't get distracted. I activate my periaudio, which is like a periscope but for the ears, and I try to pick out details. A periaudio isn't really an instrument at all. It's sort of a special attitude that makes it feel natural to notice more. They say that for a child I'm extremely sensitive—whether or not they mean it as a compliment, I don't know. They say it with a smile, but there's something sad behind that nice smile that makes me think they haven't understood much of anything. I train myself to be sensitive and my antennae tune in on their own.

I've learned that details say more than things do. If you pay attention to details, you can convince adults that everything's fine. If none of your details are wrong, they believe you.

Some examples of details that are wrong: messy hair, mucky notebooks, dog-eared books, scratches, black fingernails, dirty words.

Adults are obsessed with dirty words. Usually the words adults consider dirty aren't the ones I do.

"Stop swearing."

"They're not dirty words, it's just that things are like that!"

Take *assface:* If someone has a face that looks like an ass, with a big, ugly crack sandwiched between cheeks like a baby's butt, it's not my fault.

I also get some satisfaction from *fucking shit,* even more than from the other *fucking* swears that adults like: *fucking hell, fuckwit, fuck off,* and so on. *Fucking shit* really means *fuck* and *shit* together; it's like saying "yuck" times two, like with the dog poops you find on the pavement. The ones our neighbor's dog does are huge. You're amazed and disgusted at the same time, just like with a *fucking shit.*

Saying *piss* is for babies. Saying *stronzetta,* on the other hand, which actually means "little turd," is like sneezing, when your nose tickles and tickles. *Stronzetta* is more like Antonella, just to give you some idea. Antonella is beautiful, with long straight blond hair and dimples when she smiles—but she never smiles at you, like you're a fucking shit. My grandma always used to pinch my cheeks to give me dimples.

"Come over here and let me give you some dimples like Cary Grant."

"Leave me alone. I don't want dimples. Dimples are for babies," I shout, running around the table, tripping over chair legs, and hiding behind the wax apple in the fruit bowl, which has different levels like a wedding cake. "You'll never catch me, you old witch!"

"Don't talk to your grandma like that, you're nothing but a little brat."

"Witchy witchy witch, what a fucking bitch."

"Who taught you to speak like that?"

There are certain words adults don't like, and by now I've learned not to say them when they're around.

Adults like to use words like *in-laws, power steering, expenses, colleague, mortgage, sciatica,* and *nostalgia,* and especially words that end in *gy,* like *psychology, energy, strategy,* and *allergy.*

Mama suffers from all the *gy*s put together.

She says that psychology's no use to her, that no matter how much she sleeps she has no energy, that she has nostalgia for a time when a man was a man but all the same you need a strategy to find him or else to make more money, that with the pollen every year her allergies just explode, and that the vaccines aren't worth a damn.

As for me, I'm vaccinated against all this.

Mama complains constantly, and sometimes it's sad. But what's strange is that when she's truly sad, she stops complaining. She just drifts around the apartment, superslow and without saying a word, like a pouty angel. The other day I got a quick look at her as I walked down the hall. Her bedroom door wasn't closed all the way. She was sitting on her bed and sniffling and her eyes were red and puffy, and not because of allergies, I think. It's not pretty seeing your mama cry because you don't know how to help her, and also because you'd like to be the only one to cry at home whenever you feel like it. You're not all that big yet, so even if it's not exactly fun, you can still cry once in a while; you're allowed to, because your friends still do it. I'm jealous of my classmates, who can whine all day if they feel like it. I can't, because when Mama's so sad I can't be sadder than she is. We'd end up sinking. And we don't have a dad to save us, a fireman like one of those who after the terrorist attacks takes you in his arms and carries you far away from danger, a dad like the dads in commercials. We're always in a little bit of danger.

Mama says that Dad disappeared into the void. When she says it, she looks up over my shoulders, as if the void were still there behind me, as if she is seeing a ghost. Naturally, I turn around, but I don't see anything, just a painting of a choppy sea hanging over the sofa whose armrests are all scratched up, a yucky painting full of yucky weather with a scribbly signature in the bottom corner.

"It's impressionist," Mama explains.

I've never understood if Dad died for real or if he only died for us in the moment I came into the world. For all I know, he could be having a good time on a motorcycle with some new mama, but I don't want to ask. It doesn't seem right to butt in. I make do with the official version. It's not as if it makes such a big difference, seeing as how he's not around. Usually I try to change the subject, like when Mama asks me about school and my homework and I concentrate on my index finger and find a little strip of skin to bite off or else find a little white spot on the nail, called a *sweetheart,* which is a sign, the doctor says, of a lack of calcium. And as a matter of fact Mama doesn't like me to drink lots of milk.

So let's say I've been an orphan fatherwise more or less since the beginning. *Orphan* is the only word I hate and that adults hate too. With *orphan* we're all in agreement.

Orphan in my case is like a coat with only one sleeve.

Kids use the word *orphan* like it's a dirty word.

Adults, on the other hand, when they say *orphan* they say it under their breath, like when they talk about diseases or disasters that happen to other people. There are lots of parents who decide to split up, lots of kids who see one of their parents only once in a while; but being an orphan, that's really a nasty business, like you're missing something and everyone sees only the part that's not there. You're not what you are—you're what you're missing. Like when someone has a glass eye. You look into the eye that doesn't see, not into the healthy one that's looking at you with all it's got. Anyway, being a half orphan makes you strange; and there are things you can't do without a father.

After Mama gave me my first bicycle, she took me to the parking lot to teach me how to ride. I pedaled my first three circles, trying not to hit car bumpers or the bollards that looked like big panettones, forcing myself to keep my balance even though I was so excited. On the third circle the front tire went flat, going *pssss,* the sound of a butterfly fart, and Mama said, "Ugh, who knows how to fix a flat tire?"

And then I said, with the bike lying on the ground and my tail between my legs, "It doesn't matter, let's go home."

You get used to it, though. I'm used to it now.

Of course, when Mama acts like that, when it seems like she doesn't have a clue how it feels to have to walk home with your new bicycle, I would do anything to get her out of her "oh well" bubble, but she goes back in as soon as she can. She goes around with her nose in the air, as if she's not interested in anything. Or as if up there, on top of the houses, on top of everything, above the flat roofs and beneath the stomachache sky, where seagulls never fly, there's an answer, the solution we need, a flat-tire repairman, a Band-Aid store closed for the holiday. I feel like strangling her sometimes, I swear, but that's just an expression. I would never, ever want to become a complete orphan because then things get messed up for real. If you're a complete orphan, they take you and throw you in a home, they put a hand on your shoulder and walk you off to your cell. If you don't have a father, well, okay,

but if you don't have either one, neither a mama nor a dad,
I mean, they think it could be contagious, so they put you
in a hospital where everyone's like you, even if they know
perfectly well you can't get better. They shut you up in a
kind of hospital and you have to follow orders. You don't
have your own home anymore, or your own room. All
you've got is one fucking shit of an illness. That's also why
I pay attention to details.

I remember seeing a movie when I was little about
children like that—lots and lots of children crammed into
a building with metal camp beds with rusty bedsprings
like the ones in a prison or a mental hospital. People who
are alone for whatever reason—it doesn't matter if they're
old or young—they always end up in that kind of place because no one knows where to put people who are alone,
and so they cram them all together hoping they'll keep
one another company.

I have to admit, every once in a while Mama does try to
give me a new dad. But things never go right.

"One dad down, next one up."

She says it like she's saying she's sorry. She shrugs her
shoulders and sighs, then she pulls her neck back into her
sweater, into the shell she carries around, and then she
smiles with her eyes all bright and watery and hugs me
in a way you can see is a big effort for her, as if lifting her
arms is like lifting weights and hugging me shifts a bit
of that weight onto me. Mama acts like this joke is funny,
but I know it's not her fault if it doesn't make us laugh.

Then she usually says, "What do you say we go to bed?
Tomorrow I have to get up early."

The last dad, for example, was nice enough, but I didn't

like him because he had a scratchy beard and smelled like train seats. He seemed dirty. Actually, more than dirty, he seemed poor, and a poor dad's no good for us. If we really have to take one in, he at least has to be normal and not embarrass us. I'm sick of being different.

At school they give us lots of speeches about how we have to accept all kinds of different people: immigrant kids, handicapped kids, down-and-out kids, the ones who don't eat prosciutto or won't eat their meat rare or only eat vegetables, the kids who don't eat at all, and the ones who stuff themselves every chance they get, who've got rolls of fat on their ankles and have trouble sitting cross-legged, like my friend Chubby Broccolo from Brindisi. I'm all for it. But the fact is, I wouldn't want a strange dad. On TV there are never dads with black hairs stuck in their face like nails, dads whose job it is to wash windshields at traffic lights, dads who even in the summer wear a wind-breaker that's dirty around the collar—so why should we have to take one home with us? Mama agreed that I was right about that, even if she's sad so much of the time. Mama is too pretty for someone like that. If he kisses her too much, her face gets itchy.

"It's not a question of rich or poor, good-looking or ugly. Feelings are more complicated."

Basically, though, I know we think about it in the same way. The last few times they shut themselves up in her room to talk, she wasn't yelping anymore.

"How about if instead of a dad we get a dog?"

"I'm too tired for a dog."

"But Mama, can't you see how great it'd be, a fucking big dog who takes fucking big poops?"

I said it like that because I was mad, but weirdly she didn't yell at me. Instead she actually smiled a little and raised her right eyebrow as if she were getting an idea.

"If you want, for your birthday, you can get a cat."

So now we have Blue, who's like a cartoon cat.

We called him Blue because of his breed and also because Mama loves the blues. Ah, the blues!

"Listen. The blues are like the sound of the sea; close your eyes and they'll rock you to sleep."

Blue won't ever be a dog, but he's a great cat—he even likes Muddy Waters.

"Do you know why they called him that?" Mama asked me.

"Who?"

"Muddy Waters."

"Dunno."

"Because when he was a kid he used to play in the mud by the river and always came home covered in it."

"Lucky him."

Since we live on the eighth floor and don't have rivers or trees or other kinds of nature around us, Blue sharpens his claws on the yellow sofa. Every once in a while feathers come out of the cushions, and he thinks they're little birds. If I throw Blue crumpled-up balls of paper, he fetches them like a dog. He runs after them and ends up sliding across the floor, which makes him mad. Then he pretends nothing happened. He puts the ball on my shoe, which is funny. It's too bad I can't take him outside—as soon as I put the leash on him, he's out cold. The vet says it's narcolepsy, like the people who suddenly fall asleep because something happens to their brain, but it's nothing serious.

The vet is a nice guy. He's gentle, his eyes are big behind his glasses, and he has a little tuft of white hair in the middle of his black bangs, like a badger. He loves animals. The sleeves on his shirts are too short and you can see long hairs coming out of them, hair that's fine and soft like a wolf pup's.

"Mama, what do you think of the vet?"

"What do you mean, what do I think of the vet? Enough with your nonsense. Do I have to change the cat's doctor along with my gynecologist?"

I have to stop myself from going on or else Mama gets annoyed. When we leave the office, which smells like fur and disinfectant, all three of us feel white and shiny, all healthy and beautiful. The last time we were there, a woman with a black-and-yellow fur coat like a leopard's skin gave us really dirty looks. Her dog was dying. She glared at me for taking *A Kitten's Life* from the wobbly metal magazine tree filled with brochures about taking care of your puppy. It's not my fault I've got a fantastic kitten instead of a dog that's dying, sorry, Leopard-Coat Lady. I'm so sorry for you and especially for your dog and for the leopards you wear. Blue in his little carrier cage sticks his startled face between the bars; he's curious but also scared by the taillights and the noises of the road, hoping to be set free soon, if not in a meadow, then at least at home. You shouldn't complain about your kitten's life, Blue. After all, there are plenty who have it worse.

"But the vet is really talented, right?"

Okay, okay, let's leave it or Mama will get grumpy.

When Mama gets too grumpy, wrinkles show up on her forehead, like the lines waves leave when they come and go on the sand all day. But when her bad mood is over it's fantastic. We play together, wrestling like men do and getting into tickle fights, or else we do tongue twisters, and I always win. With me the woodchuck chucks as much wood as it can, Peter Piper's peppers are perfectly pickled, and all the animals get on just fine, woodchucks, chickens, cows, iguanas, and she who sells seashells. I'm here, have no fear, no need to worry about anything. Mama and I laugh like crazy until it's late. The next day I hope it rains, or snows, or else a tsunami comes, as long as I don't have to get up.

In the morning I think I'm on vacation and instead the alarm goes off—and keeps blaring on and on and on. What a rip-off. When Mama has nightmares, she says it's not even possible to sleep in peace in this world, and that's what I think too. Other times she says the pills have stolen her dreams, that sleep is just an inky-black nothingness, and she wakes up confused and doesn't know which way is up. Sometimes she makes coffee without putting in the water, or else the coffee.

"Don't talk to me, don't ask me for anything. I don't know anything about anything this morning."

When I get up, I get up, but inside I stay horizontal. I'm walking upright, but inside I'm still dreaming, snug as a bug in a rug, inside the second skin of my pajamas. Even my pores are like a million closed eyes. I dream about an enormous hand that gently rubs me all over. I warm myself up all on my own, while my tingling legs begin to move because obviously I'm running late.

"Hurry up."

More words adults are always saying.

"C'mon, hurry up and get a move on, we're going to be late."

They're the ones who ought to hurry. I've got all the time in the world, I tell them that. Anyway, I always get up and do everything that needs to be done. I know exactly how to do it by heart, just like I know the national anthem, "Fratelli d'Italia, / l'Italia s'è desta..." I don't need anyone to tell me how the rest goes.

1

So today I make do on my own.

Never mind that Mama hasn't gotten up. I get up anyway. I get ready on my own.

It must be because of the pills for allergies or for nostalgia, one or the other. Sometimes Mama takes a lot and sleeps more than usual. Or maybe it's narcolepsy, like what happens to the cat's brain. I should ask the vet about it.

She says that sometimes the pills have strange effects, but she also says I shouldn't worry, that everything's okay. "Sometimes I have trouble getting out of bed, but it's normal. With this cold weather who wants to be exposed to the cold, to get out from under the covers?"

Anyway, I have to get moving, and I make sure my hair's not messy before I leave. I tiptoe out to the elevator. I say hi to the man from upstairs.

"You're going to school on your own today?"
"Yes."
The elevator buttons pulse like my heart, which has

started to beat really fast, like it's trying to get out but can't.

"Yes, I do now, yes."

I act proud. Maybe I really am proud to be doing things on my own. Or maybe I'm ashamed because I'd rather be getting into the shiny car of a shiny dad with all the dad accessories. But at the same time I'm embarrassed to be embarrassed because if Dad vanished into thin air—another one of Mama's expressions—it's not our fault. Maybe she's right: Feelings are complicated, especially early in the morning. Maybe it's not important. So then I smile and clear out. That way I don't mess up.

At school, everything's normal. Everyone's ready to follow along with the lesson, despite the pillow marks on our faces, the gunk in our eyes, the yawns we barely manage to swallow. The morning carries on as usual, and as usual I pass the time by inventing stories in my head. Soon it's almost noon and my tummy begins to grumble because it's annoyed and can't take anymore. Then the bell goes. When I leave, I pretend to be in a hurry. I ask a guy out front for the time.

"Quarter past one."

I smile politely. "Are you waiting for someone?" I ask.

"Yes, my son, Giovanni. Do you know him? Perhaps he's in the same class as you?"

"No, we have some Matteos, some Davides, a Chris, and even a Samantha with an *h*, but no Giovannis."

"Do you want a lift?"

"No, thank you. I really must be going now."

Pretending to be in a hurry gives the impression that you're important. If no one is waiting for you, what do you care about being in a hurry?

The flower woman pops out of her flower hut, which stands on the corner like a guardhouse. She's ugly and smells like flower stems that have been left in the water too long, in rusty metal vases like the ones on the grave of Mama's dad, my grandpa.

"My, my, how impressive, walking home on your own now. You're quite the little man."

Why doesn't she shut up? *Little man* is another term I can't stand.

Like I can't stand the flower woman.

"What have you got against the flower woman?" Mama would ask.

"She ate the goose."

"You're still going on about the goose? C'mon, stop thinking about it."

Mama and I won a duck at the fair by throwing colored rings onto bottle necks that spun on a kind of merry-go-round. We kept it at home for a while, but then the duck turned out to be a goose and Mama gave it to the flower woman so she'd keep it at her house in the country.

"The goose will be much better off in the open air, you'll see."

The elevator is broken, or else the old man has left the doors open and it got stuck on the fifth floor, as he often does. Mama says he's got problems in his head. Sometimes she says, "Poor man." Sometimes she says, "Old fool."

It depends what pops into her head. If she's carrying groceries or bottles, she usually says "old fool."

I take the stairs: seven flights, 254 stairs. I count them

every time. Today I stop at 166. It doesn't make any sense to hurry if no one is waiting. Mama will still be in bed, dazed and sleepy. Or maybe she'll have come back around. I start climbing again, taking the steps two at a time, the even numbers, with my right foot. If I manage not to put a foot wrong, Mama will be fine for sure. I hear Blue meowing behind the door. He always does that when he hears me coming. He's happy I'm here.

Mama and Blue come toward me.

But Mama's not here. It's just Blue.

The apartment has a dark look to it. I walk straight down the seemingly endless hallway, hearing the dull thud of my steps on the carpet. After passing the row of framed drawings on the wall, old boats floating in a sea of rippled paper, I go into Mama's room. Nothing's changed.

Everything is the same as it was this morning. No movement at all.

The room is wrapped in the gray-blue half-light of winter and worn curtains. Mama is wrapped in the covers. Has she changed position or was she already hunched up like that?

What should I do?

I adjust the covers for her. She's curled up in a ball as she sleeps. Maybe she's cold.

I ask her if she wants anything.

"Are you cold, Mama? It's really cold outside, you know."

She doesn't answer.

"Please, Mama, answer me. Why don't you say anything?"

I try shaking her, but she doesn't react.

I didn't expect her to. She seems completely lost inside

herself, inside a dream so deep and far away that she's not showing any signs of life. You never know, though.

Maybe Mama is dead.

I've never seen a dead person, so I'm not sure what they look like. Actually, I did see one once beside the highway, but it was covered by a sheet, so I really only saw a sheet, and it didn't make much of an impression. All the cars slowed down to look, but there wasn't anything to see. Mama and I were going away for the weekend. So was everyone else, probably. We signaled, *tick tock tick tock,* and rejoined the flow of traffic. Mama turned on the radio; the deejay was talking bullshit. Maybe because he hadn't seen the sheet. We had the sun in our faces, a strong, cocky sun that didn't have anything to do with a dead body.

Now Mama is covered up too. The only part that's not is her face on the pillow. Her hair is messy. It looks like the hair of the woman in that famous painting that has something to do with spring, or maybe summer, but hers is like the branches of a tree that's grown upside down, like roots without the ground. What should I do? Maybe I should comb it. It's always better to have your hair tidy. What should I do? Should I wait a little longer, or ask for help right away? I can't ask for help. If Mama is dead, I can't tell anyone. If I tell, they'll take me to the orphanage.

This is terrible.

I don't want to go.

I don't want to be a complete orphan.

Anything else would be better.

Better to say that Mama's left.

Or else say nothing and act like it doesn't matter.

Better to find a way to make do. It can't be that difficult. Better to try to survive.

Better to keep it a secret and smile.

Better to use my imagination, to make myself come up with something special. Better to hope it will all just be over soon.

Better to do three thousand push-ups in a row, seven flights of stairs on one leg, long division in my head.

Better to bury Kolly the koala.

Better to think about what's better.

Better to believe that in a little bit Mama will be much better.

Is it true, Mama, that in a little bit you'll be better?

But if Mama's dead, what could be worse?

I have to pay attention to details and remember not to cry. If I start crying, I'll say that a fly flew into my eye—or no, I'll say it was a stag beetle—or else a stag deer, same thing. That way they'll think it's a joke and won't make a big deal about it

We're sitting on the bed, Blue and I, and we don't know how to act.

Blue trots back and forth and pokes his head here and there, wrinkling his nose as if he's hunting for something. He steps on the faded flowers of the bedspread, sniffs Mama, scratches with his paw, and makes a little hollow in the sheet. He gets a claw stuck and looks at me with wide-open eyes.

"I don't know what to tell you, Blue, I'm sorry. There's nothing I can do about it."

Suddenly a gigantic nothing starts to swirl and grow in my brain. My brain is a blank notebook that's never been opened, has nothing written in it, and there aren't even stories coming into my head. There aren't even lines where I can hang any words I come up with. The nothing that's flooding my head and fogging my vision won't let me do anything. A huge expanse of nothing like ice—Santa Claus has passed by, but the falling snow has wiped out his tracks. Blue has soft little pads on the bottom of his paws. He doesn't leave any tracks. The reindeer have disappeared. There are some mounds in the distance, maybe they're igloos, ice-cube houses. I feel really cold. I'm afraid of houses made of ice cubes.

Santa Claus doesn't exist. I've known that for a while. There's a white stuffed toy, a polar bear drifting on an iceberg, that doesn't know whether it'll reach land. You see the image everywhere.

I feel stuffed myself.

"Dr. Foster went to Gloucester, in a shower of rain." He stepped in a puddle and now we're all in fucking shit.

I can't call the doctor. Time passes, I don't know how much.

On autopilot, I find myself back in the living room. Blue and I squeeze up together on the sofa. Under his fur Blue is teeny-tiny. I go into my room. Blue follows me. I throw myself on the bed. I get up, go back to where I was before on the sofa. I look in Mama's dictionary for what it says under the word *death,* to see if there are details, more detailed details, something to make me understand what's happening. The dictionary is so heavy it's hard to pick up.

It says: the end of the life of a man, animal, or plant.

That's what it says, and then a dash: accidental, sudden, slow, immature—then a semicolon, etc., etc. This is to say it says nothing. It's not true that you can find answers in books.

And then to drop dead, to die a sudden death, dead

tired, extremely tired, okay. Okay, I'm dead tired too, but I don't believe I'm dead. In books people never die for real, and not in the movies either. I let the dictionary fall to the floor. It drops dead too, its pages thrown open at the letter *D* like a cowboy shot down by Indians: You've got me, you dirty bastards.

We go into the kitchen. Blue circles me like the stupid ballerina in Grandma's music box. He seems fake too. His stiff whiskers are like her lace tutu. I put a pizza in the microwave. In a few minutes the pizza heats up and comes back to life. I burn my tongue on the mozzarella, and the tip goes numb. I stick it out to show Blue, but he's not interested. He's also numb, and only wants a piece of pizza. Eating and sleeping, that's all Blue is interested in. I'll do what he does, even if I also have to go to school and do homework. If Mama is dead, I'll even have to do the grocery shopping, to bring food home for the family. I look for her purse to see if we have a little money to get by. We have a lot, actually, so there's that. There's also her bank card. I'll have to find her secret code. I'll have to practice with money because I'm not very good at it. I get confused by all the zeros, which seem like bubbles, impossible to hold on to. There's also her cell phone. I turn it off. Mama doesn't like me digging around in her bag, but I don't have a choice.

If she doesn't hurry and wake up, I just—I don't know.

If she saw me now, she'd yell at me, but she doesn't see me, doesn't think about me, doesn't want me. She couldn't care less what it means to be an orphan at my age. She's got her own problems, things I wouldn't understand. Her problems are bigger because she's bigger. I'm only a child, or an only child; it's the same thing, it just depends on how it comes out. *Sunset over the Black Sea* or the *Red Sea at Night,* depending on how you look at the painting.

I don't know what she sees. Adults can go away if they want; not me. I don't have anywhere else to go. I'm stuck here with her and her endless sleep at the end of the hall. I activate my periaudio, but I don't hear a thing; it's quiet as a grave. A periaudio is how bats hear when they're finding their way in the dark. It's a system for not smashing your face into obstacles, or at least for not doing it too hard, but this time I can't get it to work. I've got to stay with her even though she's stopped talking and listening to me. I've got to look after the cat, who's always hungry, and look after myself too.

Maybe Mama is a bitch. A bitch and an asshole. All adults are bitches and assholes. Jerks. Stinkers. Shit-heads. Idiots. Retards. Stupid assholes. Shitty, stinking assholes. Pricks. Morons. I hate them.

It's like the hate in dreams, where if you hate something you really hate it, like having jerks toss piles of fucking shit in your face, and if you like something you really like it, like whole ocean liners full of hot chocolate and whole afternoons with Antonella. I can't do anything; I hate, hate not being able to do anything. But what can I do?

Please, Mama, I'm begging you to tell me what to do.

I feel like crying. I don't know if it's right to cry, but I think in situations like this it's normal. A normal child would cry, so I cry as much as I can. No one can see me anyway. Hot water gushes from my eyes while the polar bear on its cold slab is carried away by the current.

When all of my tears run dry, I turn on the TV.

"Sometimes stupid shows help me not to think."

Let's hope Mama is right.

On TV a famous chef is giving cooking lessons. He beats eggs in front of a group of women wearing evening gowns who copy everything he does, batting their eyelashes a lot and clattering their bracelets against the pots. I could make a cake for Mama, for when she wakes up. For teatime, she says, because that's what Grandma used to say. But a cake's too complicated. Instead I'll make baked apples for her; it's not hard.

All the recipe needs is apples, sugar to taste, water, and lemon peel.

They're good to have when you feel bad. Even if the smell smells like the hospital.

I've only been in the hospital once, when I had bronchopneumonia. The nurses—old hags with scuffed shoes—came in the night and replaced my cookies with apples. Mama couldn't believe that nurses would steal a kid's cookies.

I cut each apple in fourths and sprinkle sugar over them. The apples float in the pan like icebergs, like sinking ships, like the *Titanic*. When they're ready, I pour them into a bowl, wait for them to cool a bit, and carry them in to Mama. I try not to trip on the carpet in the hall. The bowl clinks against the plate as if my hands were shaking.

I leave the bowl on her bedside table because Mama doesn't want baked apples right now.

A book called *Enduring Love* lands on the floor with a thud. Mama doesn't notice. On the cover is a picture of a hot-air balloon with people in it, rising into the sky.

The phone rings. Mama doesn't hear it.

The phone is sitting on the floor and the cord is all twisted.

"Mama went out. Yes, later. Bye."

I cross my fingers because I'm telling a lie.

"It was Giulia, Mama. Don't you want to talk to Giulia?"

Giulia is Mama's friend, the one she spends hours with complaining about everything. Giulia complains about everything too, but she's happier. It seems like she only does it to keep Mama company. They talk about men a lot, usually not nice things.

"You don't have to tell me. Remember who you're talking to," they say to each other.

A couple of Sundays ago we took a trip to the country with Giulia. Giulia's not bad even though she does have red fingernails, which I don't like.

"Look, you've got red fingernails like a chicken."

She didn't get offended. She even laughed. "That's because I *am* a chicken!"

There were chickens in the courtyard outside the restaurant where we went to eat.

"Don't touch the chickens. They're dirty. And wash your hands."

There were also different-colored rabbits, so soft you wanted to pet them.

"I'll never eat rabbit again," I swore, "never again, and not horse and not even lamb."

"Not even gelato?"

"What's gelato got to do with it? Gelato doesn't have fur."

Furry animals are my favorite. I want to have all kinds. In my opinion, people who like animals are nicer, and they understand people better too. It'd be great to be a vet and take care of the big animals, lions and leopards and cheetahs. That's what I want to do when I grow up, be a vet for big cats. We have a movie about lions that Mama and I never get tired of watching. She says she likes lions because they're strong and muscular, that when they roar they "give us an idea of infinite power," that the lion's roar is the sound of the center of the earth or of what we were before we became domesticated.

She says she'll take me to see them someday.

"When you're older, when we have more money." When whatever.

Africans say God created cats so that men could pet lions.

For now I watch the documentary. For now I've got nothing else to do.

Blue curls up near me and starts to purr.

I feel like there's too much silence in the apartment.

When there's too much silence, it makes more noise than noise does, like the deaf kids I meet on the tram sometimes. They're going to the deaf school, where they can understand one another with hand gestures, but on the way there they make a ton of crazy sounds and you don't have any choice but to listen. If one of them gets his ticket jammed in the machine, he might as well have a fish bone stuck in his throat.

Silence, on the other hand, fills up your head like the blank notebook, and it's too big to do anything about it.

There's a time just before dinner, before the day ends, when you feel the silence more strongly. At most there are cars going by and quickly zooming away. They're inside the life that's outside, beyond our window, beyond the television screen; they're part of the noise of TV shows, of things that happen far away. Then usually Mama gets home and starts messing with dinner. Even if I'm in my room I can hear the noises coming from the kitchen, cupboards slamming, the mosquito buzz of the electric can opener, a metallic rumble through the silverware drawer. It's over, I tell myself, it's all over. We're safe. I go to her. I circle around her like a tsetse fly. Tsetse flies are torture for lions too. Lions sleep two-thirds of the day and wake up in the evening to eat. Since it's winter it gets dark early; it's already pitch-black at five.

Every two minutes I feel like going into her room to see if something's happened, if Mama has tasted the baked apples, but I'm afraid of finding out that she hasn't even touched them and being disappointed.

Better to wait for evening; during the winter evening comes soon.

Patience is a virtue, fine, I get it. I've got all the time in the world.

Inside my eyes there's nothing but blackness. When I open them everything is dark.

I fell asleep, I feel cold; the movie's finished. Rain taps on the window, otherwise it's quiet. The shapes of the furniture are the backs of elephants in the savanna. The dark stain of the painting looms over my head.

Even Blue is snoring. Every so often he makes a sucking sound. Maybe he's dreaming about sucking milk, because in dreams milk doesn't give him the runs; salami doesn't cause spots, nostalgia, melancholy...The great thing about cats is that even when they grow up they stay kittens. Blue always tries to get some milk when I have breakfast, but I can't give it to him because milk upsets his tummy. One time he threw up on Mama's bed and she had to put everything in the washing machine.

"I swear I'll throw the cat in too."

She wasn't being serious, though, just joking.

I've got a nasty taste in my mouth, like I ate something rotten. Maybe I'm sick too, like Mama. And I won't wake up again. I cross the room like a sleepwalker, shuffling with my arms out in front of me as I look for the light switch. I turn on all the lights. I turn the TV back on. I turn everything on, the stereo and the radio too; that way the apartment seems full of people.

I go into Mama's room; she's still turned off.

I look for a detail that will tell me she's moved. I don't know . . . maybe her hair. I don't think so. I wonder if she was exactly like this before. I call her name, shout at her, pinch her. Nothing. I feel my face getting wet again, feel like I can't swallow, feel my legs wobble, and my chin and my voice. I feel something hot in my stomach. She doesn't feel anything anymore. I really think she is dead.

I curl up next to her. The pillow gets flooded. I stay like this until I realize it's not possible to stay like this forever. When I go into the bathroom, my eyes are red, my face looks like I've got the flu. I pick up the toothpaste and squirt some in my mouth, without the toothbrush, to get rid of the disgusting taste that's all over my tongue. I feel sick, like I've just turned one hundred thousand corners in the car, hurtling down a Russian mountain that's like a roller coaster.

I'm still cold. Maybe I've got a temperature. In the living room everyone's shouting: the guy on the news, the radio announcer, Jovanotti singing. It's raining, really raining. When Mama wants to see if I have a temperature, she puts her lips to my forehead, but I can't do that to myself. Fucking shit. I take the thermometer from the medicine cabinet, shake it up and down, and put it under my arm. Then I change my mind—there's no point in having a fever now. I lean my forehead against the edge of the sink; it's nice and cool. I stay bent over for another two or three centuries, until my back starts to hurt like an old person's. Blue's standing in the doorway. He looks at me but doesn't understand. He tries to meow, but nothing comes out. Even he doesn't know what to say.

It was only a little while ago that I woke up, but I'm really tired. I should do my homework, but I don't know if I'm up to it. Someone whose mother has just died can't do homework, but that isn't an excuse, because I can't tell anyone about it. It has to stay a secret, a really big secret just between us. I don't want to end up in an orphanage.

When I was younger Mama used to read me a story about a little girl who was left in an orphanage. At night the girl would hide under the covers, even though they scratched her face. She was sad because nobody loved her. Then she was saved by a friendly giant who ate only snozzcumbers. He came through the window and carried her away. She stopped being just one orphan in a thousand and became the daughter of a big, strong man. But I stopped believing in giants—whether I liked it or lumped it, as Mama would say—a long time ago.

I have to do my homework. I can't risk them suspecting anything.

There was one boy at school who told a story about how he hadn't done his homework because his aunt had died—then they discovered it wasn't true at all and made him go to a million appointments to figure out how he'd ended up telling such a whopper. He earned an unsatisfactory grade for behavior. His aunt was pretty upset about it, especially because she wasn't decrepit at all.

The telephone rings. I run to turn off the noise. It's Giulia again.

"My mother said she'll call you tomorrow, she's cooking."

"No worries, I'm leaving, going on vacation, God willing. I'm already at the airport. I'll be back in a few weeks. Say good-bye to your mother and give her a kiss for me, and be good."

"I will. Send us a postcard."

Giulia says good-bye in a voice that's so happy it's gross. She doesn't notice anything. She's got other stuff on her mind.

Eating is disgusting. I don't think I'll ever eat again. I don't know what to do. It's my first dinner without a good dinner, my first night without a good night. For the first time in so long, maybe ever. I'll have to get used to doing without Mama. When she grazes my cheek it seems less like a kiss than a warmish breath of air, bringing me luck. I decide to sleep on the sofa. So long to my room, to the toys scattered across the floor, to the bears on the shelf secretly looking and laughing at me.

"You're nothing but a race of stupid, weak bipeds."

So long to all the things I'm leaving behind.

The only one I take is the koala.

"What do you think?"

Kolly doesn't answer. He must be offended because ever since I got Blue I've stopped asking him for his opinion.

Old Kolly is made from real koala fur, with a brown nose that's always cold. Someone Grandma knew in Australia sent it to me.

"I was very fond of this friend, you know. He was tremendously handsome when he was young, and an amazing dancer as well, but then he went away and I haven't seen him since."

At that point Grandma was already off on a tangent that filled her mouth with the words *fond, friend, Australia* . . . Australia like Asturias or Austria-Hungary, strange places on a map that went out of date a hundred wars ago, the Australia of "My dear, dear boy, it's on the other side of the world. When it's dark here, the sun's up there; when it's winter here, it's summer there."

The Australia of kangaroos and duck-billed platypuses.

And then Mama, who never wants to go away anywhere, says, with a swoosh that sounds like a wingbeat: "And birds of paradise, can you imagine? It must be paradise on earth. Maybe we should all go off to Australia, every last one of us."

Who knows if Kolly would like to go back to his part of the world and climb eucalyptus trees.

"What do you say, Kolly? Would you like to go visit your relatives on the other side of the world?"

We could also go sleep with Mama, but if she's really dead I'm not sure I want to be close to her. If she's dead she's already an angel. She'll come and visit me without my even hearing her steps on the wooden floor, without running into the furniture, without hurting herself on the corners. She'll come in her silk nightgown and, like a guardian angel, make it so that I dream in color. She'll slide along without touching the ground, like a rapper. I don't know anymore if guardian angels exist. They tell you so many whoppers with the excuse that you'll like the stories, but you're never completely sure if they're true or not. Or maybe Mama'll transform into a zombie. I feel like a zombie myself now, but Mama is too beautiful to become a monster. She's never a monster, even when she gets mad and makes a nasty face. Eventually it passes and she goes back to being nice. She's nice now too, it's just that she forgot to wake up.

Grown-ups forget so much. Especially among themselves. They'll see each other for a while, they'll call each other, they'll chat, say "my dear," "my darling," and then forget each other.

"Sometimes people just fall into oblivion."

Oblivion is like a long hallway but vertical, a hole like the one on the landing we throw trash down, with scratchy cement walls and a shiny gray hatch like a sulky mouth. People fall into the hole, plop, and then stay there, squashed one on top of the other, waiting until someone wonders whatever happened to them.

"For example, do you remember that one guy, what was his name? Who knows whatever happened to him?"

That one guy, like my father, or maybe it is my father.

I think Mama and I have fallen into someone's oblivion too, because people don't seek us out so much, maybe because she's sad, and when she's sad she's not much fun. You've really got to love her to put up with her then. Only if it's your own mother can you be fine with it—you can't do anything else, she's the only one you've got.

We've definitely fallen down the dads' memory holes,

my real dad's and the other ones' as well, the contenders'. Now it really seems like everyone has forgotten everything, that the world is far, far away, like in science-fiction movies where you see Earth from another planet.

I'm sure there's lots of life on other planets, it's just that we're light-years away here in the megagalaxy of the eighth floor. There are lights in the windows across the street, people carrying dishes from the dining room to the kitchen, TVs that flicker with a bluish light, but we've lost touch, even Mama says so.

"You know how it is, in this city it's so easy to lose touch."

It would take a super–remote control to beam yourself into those living rooms where big families eat popcorn in front of a good movie, where they celebrate real Christmases with great big Christmas trees that touch the ceiling with their golden tips.

I hate Christmas because none of this ever happens. I hate the candied fruit in the panettone, I hate the crooked figurines in the nativity scene in the school lobby, and I hate the fat priest with the sticky hands who wants to bless me.

"Go with God, my son."

"No, thanks, if you're coming too."

It always turns out I get sadder because I'm supposed to be happier. I can't wait for Christmas to be over so that I don't have to think about it anymore.

There are presents, of course, but they're not always enough.

"Aren't you going to unwrap your gifts? That one with the red bow is from me; the lilac-colored one is from Grandma; that one with the airplane paper is from Giulia. Merry Christmas, my pet."

Already the day after Christmas is better.

And tomorrow will already be better too. Maybe tomorrow things will be different, my pet. All I have to do is make tomorrow come soon.

I bring the quilt with the clouds onto the sofa, along with Blue and the koala. The alarm clock quietly beams green Martian codes my way. I try to close my eyes.

It's strange to sleep with the light on, but I don't feel like turning it off tonight; it's better this way. On the inside of my eyelids I see swarms of microbes crazily moving about, like when you look into a microscope and spot the ones responsible for who knows what disease; or when you stare at a clear sky when it's really, really clear, inhabited only by millions of quote marks without words, without explanations, without motives.

At Grandma's house, where it's dark even during the day, when the sun comes through the shutters, the dust particles do a dance in the air, glittering like metallic paint. A ray of cosmic dust, penetrating the lazy half light of the afternoon, a sword that shimmers with all the colors of the rainbow and grants special powers, makes me a secret knight of the great disorder's higher order, a master cherry-stone spitter.

Deep in darkness, there was also the music room, with its armchairs covered with ghost sheets, the coatrack covered in ghosts' overcoats, and the forgotten instruments that no one used anymore but that absolutely no one was allowed to touch.

"Practice on this," Grandma would say, handing me a mandoline so that I could slice the hard-boiled eggs.

The piano was opened only for my grandfather's funeral. Grandma sat down on the upholstered stool, stiffly erect, her eyes bright from crying or from too many toasts in her husband's honor: "A good man after all."

She began to play military marches, bobbing her purple hair from side to side, maybe in celebration of finally having become the supreme commander of the whole shebang. My grandmother has purple hair, a detail that has always really made me laugh.

hear an ambulance siren, coming closer and closer. It's here. It's parked in the living room or under the bed. It's deafening me. I stick my fingers in my ears, but it's no use, the noise continues. I wake up in a sweat. The alarm clock bores into my sleep like the drill they used to break up the street down below. I fling a heavy arm out of bed to turn it off. It was only a bad dream. Everything's all right. Then I remember. Nothing's all right. Not one single thing. What am I doing here on the sofa?

Mama didn't get up this morning either.

There's too much silence now that I've turned off the siren and the jackhammer that were hollowing out my head.

Mama's not getting up anymore.

Now I remember everything.

I sit up to think about my new situation. I look at the living-room furniture; it's familiar and strange at the same time, like being in a hotel or at someone else's house. Blue gets his purr motor running.

I have to find some courage.

I don't have any.

I'm in a daze, sitting on the sofa with my legs and arms open wide, waiting for another pair of arms to pick me up, to pose me like she used to for baby pictures, a naked, confused newborn in the middle of the bed, like the picture of Grandpa when he was young, a chubby little grandfather dressed up in frills, looking nothing like the bony old man I knew.

I tell my feet to shake off this daze, tell my legs to carry me down the hall to see how things are going, tell my head to be a bit more positive. But they're not listening.

At times like these it's usually Mama who comes to get me moving.

Now I have to get myself moving. I tell myself I have to get used to it: "You've got to get used to it. You've got to manage. You can't be afraid of going down the hall."

I argue with myself out loud.

"Mama's never frightened you before; she can't frighten you now. Can't you see she can't even move?"

She is still still.

Extremely still.

Nothing can be done. There's only one hope—that she'll be resurrected, like Jesus. After three days. We've just begun the second, and who knows if it's true that Jesus was resurrected. They say he was, but I don't know if I believe it. Even Grandpa didn't really believe it was possible to go into and rise back out of graves, and anyway, when he died, he wasn't resurrected; he just died, and that was that. He wanted a glass of wine on his grave instead of flowers. Mama said he'd been in the war and seen so many dead people that he stopped believing in God and all those religious stories, because in this world there is no religion. Looking at all the people who die for no reason—I'm not just talking about bad people but good ones too—it's hard to believe that there's an invisible someone protecting us. I'm not particularly interested in these things, even if now I could really use a God or some such thing to give me a hand. If there was one, this would really be the time to prove it.

He could tell me what to wear to school. It has to be a clean shirt, because Mama would never send me to school with yesterday's shirt—actually, he could wake up Mama, if he can. I can't. But God probably has more important things to do.

I have to wash as well. If I was sure Mama was going to be back today, I wouldn't bother, but since I'm not, I can't risk them noticing anything strange on account of details, like the ones that betray people in *Columbo*. Lieutenant Columbo always looks rumpled just so everyone will underestimate him. Obviously, if he was the suspect he'd change his raincoat.

I put on a striped shirt; it'll do fine. And a green sweater. I wash my armpits but forget the bidet—who cares, it's not like anyone's going to be inspecting my underwear.

"If you don't wash below too, you'll have moss and lichens growing there, like in the taiga and the tundra."

Mama always exaggerates.

Blue licks himself to get clean. I'm so jealous. Blue has eighteen whiskers per side and long hairs like whiskers above his eyes. When I don't have anything else to do, I count them, to see if there happen to be any more, since Blue is growing up too; no longer a kitten, as the flower woman would say, but becoming quite the little cat.

"Okay, Blue, time for din-dins."

Din-dins is Blue's favorite word. If you say it to him, he gets all excited and begins to follow you around and won't stop until you give him something. Blue jumps on the table, slips past the box of cereal, the sugar, and the glass ashtray from Venice that's a bit chipped on one side, and launches himself at the can of mackerel as if he hasn't seen food for I don't know how long. A bit later, in all his enthusiasm, he pushes his bowl under the sideboard and then looks at me in surprise, as if to say: "Help! Where'd my din-dins go?"

Cats do things like that. They're really intelligent and sometimes stupid. They understand everything, but when it comes to food they know nothing.

Blue rubs himself all soft and silky against my legs. I'd like to have a sleeping-bag body like Blue and snuggle down inside myself and pull up the zipper. I'd also like to have a tail and wag it when I'm cross, make it bristle when I meet assfaces, and hold it straight up when I'm happy and feel like walking with my head high.

Maybe I'd like to be Blue. Who can go back to purring with Mama.

"Did you feed Blue?"

Usually, before going out, Mama asks me: "Did you feed Blue?"

She only asks to bug me, because she knows very well whether I've done it or not. If I go back to show her the bowl, she says: "Hurry up."

If I hurry, she says: "Get a move on."

Before leaving I check up on Mama but without going into her room. I look at her from far away. I'm in a rush.

• • •

the first true lie

45

I have to run. Whenever I do, the corners of the books in my backpack poke my back. I've got to tighten the straps, or else leave the house sooner next time and then walk normally.

It's freezing cold; when I breathe I can see my breath. If I can see my breath, it means I'm alive, even if I'm dying of cold.

It's the coldest winter since 1900-something and it's windy too, which it almost never is. The wind helps with the pollution; it reduces the fine particles, the sneakiest ones, the ones that get in everywhere without anyone seeing them and then make you sick.

Luckily, we don't live far from school.

We're 3,700 steps away, more or less, because every time I count them the number is different.

I run into Davide at the entrance—just as well—we'll come in together.

Inside, along the corridor with all the drawings pinned up, there's a sign that says NO RUNNING.

I ask Davide if he believes in God, and he replies: "Are you stupid or what?"

And we rush to class.

I realize I've asked Davide a pretty odd question, out of the blue and so early in the morning. I've got to be careful not to let strange stuff like that slip out.

"Do you see this? It's a piece of granite that's become part of my hand. It's my rock hand. Touch it."

My deskmate has scabs on his hands because yesterday he popped a wheelie on his skateboard and landed in the gravel. He picks at the clotted blood on his knuckle and gets blood on his exercise book. The blood doesn't stop. It spreads over the page and Mrs. Squarzetti panics, fearing a hemorrhage.

"Oh my God, a hemorrhage!"

Rock Hand is taken downstairs to have his war wounds tended to. Later Rock Hand will sport a new Band-Aid.

I like Band-Aids a lot. I put them on even when I haven't hurt myself at all. Sometimes I'll draw on my skin a little bit to make it look more real. Band-Aids give the impression of an adventurous life, of someone who falls down but doesn't really hurt himself.

"What'd you do to yourself?"

"It's nothing, just a little karate chop. I broke seven bricks with a single blow."

"No way!"

The incident with my deskmate is the most exciting event of the morning.

When Antonella sees blood, her face goes all twisty as if she's going to pass out. I feel like throwing up because real blood turns my stomach, but I hold out: It's just the soul of the red Bic pen gushing everywhere because I've swallowed the cap again. I think about my heavenly soul that may not even exist. I look at Antonella's heavenly blue eyes. She gets more beautiful every day and I blush just at the thought that she could be looking at me.

I hold out even though feeling sick makes me think of a memory from nursery school: little spaghetti hoops floating like life preservers in a pool of tomato sauce; a kid who's honking like an elephant and the next thing he's up at the blackboard throwing up his cafeteria lunch, and it's making people laugh but also throw up themselves; the smell of vomit stays in my nose even afterward, even now.

I hate pasta with tomato sauce. If there must be sauce, at least let it be on the side, without everything mixed together. With things like that, if you meet with the school psychologist he or she will tell your parents you've been traumatized, as if you've discovered you've only got one parent instead of two, or your mama's sleeping with someone else's dad.

"Childhood trauma."

It's just smaller, when it comes to pasta with tomato sauce.

In any case I hold out. I don't want everyone to see what I've eaten for breakfast: a bowl of dry cereal that looked exactly like Blue's cat food. I swallow and it tastes like acid and also like yogurt, even though the yogurt was already gone this morning. I licked the container and tried to reach the bottom with my tongue. I cleaned the tinfoil lid until all I tasted was tinfoil, the kind that shocks your back teeth.

Outside it's started raining again, and it's not the good rain anymore, the impressive kind. It's a useless kind of rain that makes you sleepy and the outlines of things fuzzy, and makes you think it will never stop.

It's raining like that inside me too.

Usually when I'm bored in class I read under my desk, or draw, or go over Mama's words in my head, trying to discover their secrets. Nostalgia: tender, burning desire for people, places, and things she'd like to return to. Sciatica: extreme pain in the sciatic nerve that doesn't let her go skiing. And so on. I invent private exercises, count the holes the woodworms have worm-eaten out of the window frames over the centuries and centuries, amen, so the hours go by faster.

Sometimes I pay attention with one part of my brain, and with the other I daydream. I imagine that past the roof and the chimneys and the TV antenna, there are the sea and the clear sky and ships with pirates. Pirates don't hunt whales; they hunt the people who hunt whales. The pooping pigeons on the windowsill are albatrosses perched on the ship's main yard. I don't tell anyone I can do it because adults don't think it's so easy. They think you have to do one thing at a time, that you can't talk and eat, put on pants and walk, draw and learn, dream and stay awake. If I think about something totally different, I just have to pay attention to where my eyes wander, otherwise it seems like I'm seeing ghosts, like Mama when she says that Dad vanished into thin air and she stares at the painting with the nasty weather.

At home, whenever I can't stand it anymore, I close myself in the wardrobe that no one ever opens. I sit on top of the drawers in the middle of the clothes that smell like mothballs, herringbone overcoats and the cloth sacks I used to take to nursery school, blue and white checked with my name embroidered on them, still smelling like bread and chocolate. I stay there and think for a bit, with the old overcoats on my face. I might cry if I really have to, and wipe my snot with the sleeve of an old shirt. Then I get over it, and then I don't want Mama to worry too much.

Mama. Mama. Mama.

The memory of Mama explodes again in my head.

A geyser of fear. I'm so afraid that someone will notice something.

Do you know what the doctor said to the skeleton who showed up for an appointment? I write it on a piece of paper and I pass it to Davide.

He shakes his head.

I write it on another piece of paper. Couldn't you have come earlier?

Out of the corner of my eye I can see him laugh.

I'm safe.

Everything's okay.

When we get out it's pouring.

Needles of freezing rain everywhere. I forgot to bring a hat. To stay out of it I'm forced to pass close to Assface. It's a chance I have to take because I can't risk getting sick. I cross my heart and hope to die he doesn't say it again:

"Orphan-orphan-orphan." He repeated it like an evil chant.

Not too long ago, on Columbus Day, I'll never forget it; I was with my friends and Assface said: "Orphan-orphan-orphan."

And I thought, Now I'm gonna smash that assface of yours.

"Assface in the first degree."

And before I thought, No, maybe better not, I'd punched his nose, right there in the middle of that big ugly crack. I didn't know how, but my arm had been faster than my thoughts, a solid hit before I'd even realized it myself, as if my body had decided to seek justice on its own.

Notebooks had gone flying to the ground, shedding pages like trees in autumn, and suddenly I was shedding the old image of myself and speaking openly to Assface, whose eyes goggled like someone who can't believe his own eyes, his own ears, his own runny nose.

"You'll pay for this."

"Sure I will. Let this be a lesson to you, Assface."

I had muttered it to myself while the others stood by speechless in admiration; suddenly I felt six inches taller.

But now I can't react at all; I have to be careful not to draw attention to myself. I speed up. Assface pretends not to see me and yet I pass so close to him that I can count one by one his moles, like pistachios in his nasty mortadella face. I speed up and I'm past him. Almost home.

Mama's still sleeping, buried between the pillows.

Seeing her like that in the big bed, she seems smaller. Still the same expression, it's just that her face is darker. When I touch her, she seems colder. But it's cold outside too. I put a coat over her, and two coins fall out of one of the pockets.

If people are happy, they don't die like this, just by chance.

Maybe they die in an accident, but not in their sleep.

Maybe Mama died of heart problems, because no one could love her enough, not even me. Maybe I wasn't able to make her stay in my life, to make her live for me, at least. Maybe I'm not worth much at all, not for her, not for anyone.

I take off my shoes with this new idea spinning in my head. I hurl one shoe here, another one there. Blue is scared. He makes his tail big so that it looks like that contraption for getting rid of spiderwebs. One shoe ends up under the sofa. I've got all kinds of titicaca in my socks. I have to accept my responsibilities.

What are my responsibilities?

Keep my room clean, check to make sure the cat is okay, change his litter, study, don't say "fucking shit" all the time, be sure the gas is off if I've used the oven. Do what I need to do so there isn't food between my teeth.

Don't be an extra bump in the road when the going gets tough.

Understand that grown-ups have grown-up problems.

Adults have no idea how many strategies kids have to come up with to be what they are. Sometimes they tell you to stop acting like a child, other times that it doesn't matter because you're just a child ... but what a beautiful child! What a little man! I think about the little hanger-men who hold up the clothes in the wardrobe that smells like mothballs. Because I close myself in there I might become a little hanger-man myself, with bony shoulders and a question-mark head. Who knows.

In any case, even adults don't always know what they're saying.

"I'm drawing a blank."

Or:

"Funeral for the deceased."

Who else would it be for?

I go into my room to look for my slippers, the ones with the moose antlers on them that Mama gave me for Christmas. Blue's chewed on them, so now one horn is leaking yellow cotton wool, like the stuff they put up your nose when it's bleeding. Like when I got hit in the face with a soccer ball and they took me to the emergency room. Mama thought it was a concussion and was more upset than I was, but the doctor told her it was nothing.

As I slipper across the room, Blue tries to grab what's

left of the antler. On TV, the chef is still there, sur-
rounded by dressed-up women being all over-the-top—
I zap them. In the kitchen, the table and the floor are
covered with dry food; I forgot to put the box away and
Blue has scattered them everywhere. The sink is full of
dirty dishes. On the windowsill there's a plant Mama
calls a succulent, a gift from someone or other, made up
of two kinds of spiny cucumbers, one tall and one short.
It survives even without water, like us. We're succulents
too, shut up in the apartment. If you touch it, it stings in
self-defense.

The apartment like this makes me sick.

It's not like when you're alone for a day and you do what
you want and what you usually can't. Now I can do everything and I don't feel like doing anything. I'm so free
my head spins just thinking about it. I'm free and I'm a
prisoner at the same time, like hamsters who spin their
wheels and stay in the same place. They spin and spin and
don't go anywhere.

If I stop for a moment, the blank notebook comes back
into my head and I can't even imagine. It's horrible because it's thanks to daydreams that I've always made it
through okay. Teachers say I have a vivid imagination.

"Imagination is a great resource in times like these.
Perhaps you're unaware of this because you don't read
newspapers, but at times reality is stranger than fantasy. So it becomes necessary to be even more fantastic in
order to make it in life."

But now I don't know what to imagine.

I try to imagine that this is happening to someone else,
because it's a bit like that: I'm inside what's happening

but also outside. I want to disappear but at the same time I don't. I don't feel like shutting myself up in the wardrobe anymore because now everything is like a closed wardrobe, but also like an open one—there's no point in hiding inside the apartment anymore. I can whine and wipe my nose on the tablecloth, the napkins, my pajamas, the curtains in the living room. Everything is old. It all smells like an old wardrobe. Wide open and sealed shut at the same time. I can do everything and I don't want to do anything—I only want to go back to how it was. I bury my nose in the last piece of toilet paper. I make myself a Nutella sandwich. The bottle of milk is empty. I drink tap water, which tastes like chlorine.

During the winter the days are short, but today seems to go on forever and ever.

I don't even know if I should give up hope or not.

"Hope is the last to die."

Or the second to last?

Mama seems more and more dead.

I should study the history of hominids, those slouching, hairy creatures in our textbooks, walking in single file until one straightens up and marches ahead like a soldier, *forward* march.

With a hominid around maybe Mama would feel less lonely.

"Why is it you can't make up your mind to find a decent man? I say this for your son's sake as well, because you can't do it all alone."

"I'm tired of falling in love, tired of falling out of love, tired of fucking. I don't even remember how to make love anymore."

"That's love! Right now things seem one way to you,

but that's not necessarily the way things are. Look at me, I've been falling in and out of love since I was fifteen. Every time, I say never again, may I be struck down if I fall for it again. Then I meet another one and it's another round, another race. If you find one who knows what he's about, you'll see how quickly you'll change your mind."

"No, for me it's different. To fall in love you need to want it, and I just want to sleep."

Mama lights another cigarette and curls a lock of hair around her finger. Giulia just sits there with her nose in the air, contemplating the smoke as it curls around itself, in search of inspiration or else the right moment to slip away.

Sometimes Giulia invites her out to dinner with friends and Mama invents an excuse, which is usually me.

"Sorry, this evening I really have to stay home with him. You know how he is . . ."

Other times Mama says she suffers from loneliness:

"Loneliness is a whistling that worms itself into your head. It's the echo of ships that have already sailed, that you can no longer reach, not even if you swim."

She told me:

"Once a ship or a train departs, there's nothing else you can do. You're left gazing after a gleam of light on the horizon, slowly fading into the fog, the way a memory fades into the dull gray of the present."

She said:

"That's how I feel, like I'm on the shore, or in an empty station, having arrived to life too late."

Mama feels lonely even though she's never alone, because I'm always here with her; but it must not be enough. In order not to feel so lonely she went to talk to a man with a beard who listened to her once a week in a house full of books that were full of complicated ideas. I flipped through a few of them while I was in the waiting room. I wonder, though, what do you get out of paying someone to listen to you, to care for you?

I care for her for free, but it must not be enough.

It may be that she doesn't want to confess her darkest thoughts to me directly. Sometimes she writes them down using tiny, tiny letters, then forgets the pieces of paper on the kitchen table; or else she talks about them to somebody in a low voice. She talks slowly and she moves slowly.

She did it the other night too.

At times Mama moves in slow motion.

When she slows down more than usual she decides not to go to work for a few days.

"One of these days they'll end up firing me."

I think one of these days came.

So she took a day or two to sleep.

When normal people don't work they go on vacation.

Last year even Mama took a week for a real vacation, and we went to Venice.

"Do you know that if you go to Venice with a man before you're married, then you won't ever marry him? It happened to me once."

Or more than once.

More than a city, Venice seems like one of those books with three-dimensional objects that pop out of the pages, suddenly spreading out before your eyes. You turn the corner and you feel as if you're turning a page, as if you're falling into another fantastic story. Venice is all hand-drawn. The houses are ancient and every detail seems specially designed by an architect in a wizard's hat. There are no cars and you can walk everywhere. Gondolas slip by on the water, each one steered by a single sailor with a striped shirt like mine.

Mama and I took a ride around like the couples do.

"Don't you think this city's magical? Isn't it incredible that places like this still exist in the world?"

We went to visit the churches and the museums with their paintings that are hundreds of years old, where you have to whisper so you don't disturb the other people; we also discovered a special place under an arch where everyone sticks their gum. We stopped and played under the portico of a palazzo on the canal: If you walk around the base of one of the columns without falling, you get to make a wish. Almost nobody makes it, but it's fun to try.

"Don't say it, don't tell me the wish. If you say it, then it won't come true."

We bought a glass ashtray and sat at a little café table with the glittering sea in front of us and to one side a church with a golden ball on top. We wrote postcards: to Giulia, to Grandma, to Davide and Chubby Broccolo, plus I sent Antonella the one with a gondola. I wrote "Greetings from Venice"—I wanted to write "I love you" but was too embarrassed.

We had some really good gelato. It was like a bar of chocolate dipped in whipped cream. The waiter recommended it to us and Mama said: "Sure, let's try it.

We're on vacation, and it's always a good idea to try the local specialty."

It must be wonderful to live in a place like Venice. I wonder how it would have been if my stork had been rerouted and I'd been born in Venice.

"In winter, though, Venice is depressing."

So no, then, I think it's better how it is, for us to be where we are.

Mama says that in winter Venice is like a cold: The world outside is even more muffled and far away, and your head pounds for no reason while your nose runs, like those stray cats with heart-shaped noses that nobody has the heart to clean.

But the thing I remember most about Venice is that it's either extremely noisy or extremely quiet. You're either walking in the middle of millions of people who are stepping on your feet and getting stuck in the really narrow streets or on the bridges, everyone's shouting in different languages and the gondoliers are singing and the boats' motors are roaring, and there's always someone hammering somewhere or a radio going or people calling out to each other from one place to another; or else you take a random turn and maybe you find an open space with nobody there, and the only thing you can hear is the water in the canals and the echo of your own footsteps and the calls of seagulls chasing one another. It's like suddenly being in another world, but all this happens by chance, because you don't really know where you are, you're just lost again. It's a happy silence, though, not like the one now.

. . .

I'm listening to the silence when suddenly my periaudio picks up a signal: a shuffle of footsteps behind the door. Waves of blood crash in my head, whipping up a storm. I listen some more: There's someone moving around. I hear a creak like when Mama gets out of bed and scrapes her feet on the ground in search of her slippers, which is like the flapping of a moth caught inside a lampshade.

It can't be true. I hope so much that it is true. I hope with all my might that it's Mama, Mama who's finally decided to get up and return to us. Like the people who remember their entire past life a moment before they die, in a second I see the rest of my life to come, now that we're about to go back to living. Like when I heard a friendly, cracking voice booming from the apartment next door and hoped it wasn't our neighbor but someone much nearer, the nearest kind of neighbor, one who sings in the shower or while shaving, sings love songs or opera for Mama but also for me.

I listen again.

The noises become clearer. I make out two voices, voices of people I don't know. The neighbor who loved opera moved away two years ago.

I pray to Mama for it to be true, but it's not true.

The noises aren't coming from Mama's room. There's someone muttering behind the front door.

I don't even have time to think before I hear someone ringing the doorbell.

Once, twice.

Who could it be at this hour? How did they get into the building? How'd they find me out? I've been silent as a mouse the whole time.

I hold my breath as I put my eye to the peephole, as slowly as I can, like a burglar in reverse, one who's afraid of being discovered living in his own apartment.

I see two decrepit old women, all bundled up against the cold. Blue starts to meow.

"We're Jehovah's Witnesses. Is anyone home?"

"No, it's just a cat. Let's go."

3

Today Antonella has a ponytail.

And a hair clip shaped like a ladybug. If a ladybug lands on you, it's a sign of good luck. I'd like to be older, to be able to go to the movies with her alone, to sit in the back row and give her a kiss. Usually when I think of something impossible, it distracts me, and then everything goes back to normal: peace, amen.

But today's different.

It's like with a toothache. If it goes away for five minutes it seems like you never had it at all. But then the pain yanks you back, and it seems like all you have is teeth, like you're just one giant tooth and you can't think of anything else. You become your tooth; nothing else is important to you. You'd like to have dentures and put them in a glass on the bedside table like Grandpa did. The dentures smile all on their own and you don't have to think about it anymore. You don't even have to try.

It's like the rain, the kind of rain that gives you no hope it'll ever stop.

The trees have disappeared in some kind of fuzzy mist. They're plane trees, the kind that drivers smash into.

Chubby Broccolo is looking out the window too.

Chubby is great, but never ask him for a bite of his sandwich.

Chubby's real name is Francesco, but only the grown-ups call him Francesco, when they have to tell him off.

Mama says that obese children will have millions of problems when they grow up. I'm not obese, but I have millions of problems right now.

I think I'm fairly good-looking, because everyone says so.

"You're the spitting image of your mother."

Davide asks me if I'll go to the movies with him that afternoon.

"It's Elisabetta's birthday, so we're all going to the movies."

"I'd like to. I'll call you after lunch."

"Will your mother let you?"

"I think I can convince her."

"I'll tell my mother to call yours," he says.

Fucking shit, I think.

"Okay," I say.

I'll make up something later, I think.

It's hard to behave so that no one knows anything, when they really don't know anything.

With one part of my brain I listen to the lesson about hominids, all the stages of the evolution of man leading up to *Homo sapiens*, which are us now. With the other part I think of a solution, because I'd like to go to the movies; if nothing else it would distract me.

I don't even know if I really want to go to the movies

with them, but I do want everything to be normal. And it would be normal to go to the movies with Davide and his pain in the ass of a sister.

I wonder what it's like to have a sister and if it's better to have an older or a younger one, like Elisabetta. I've thought about it so many times without reaching any conclusion. There are pros and cons.

Right now, for example, it would be a disaster. Sisters don't know how to keep their mouths shut, because they're girls and they think they know how to do everything. Davide's sister is always butting in, always acting like she knows more about things than you do. Then if you figure out that seven times eight equals fifty-six before she does, she starts to scream the house down because she can't stand losing. When she makes cookies, we all have to eat them and they're awful, superhard, like a nougat bar without the nougat flavor. It's like munching on a pencil, and I hate pencils, even when they're shaped like cookies. I hate pencils because even if you erase what you've written, there'll always still be a dark mark underneath. Then again, if I had a smart, well-trained sister, a sister who was all mine, it would be better because at least then I'd have someone to talk to.

I can't decide about this sister thing. Maybe a brother would be better, I don't know. But even then it would depend on the brother. Maybe a twin—a twin would definitely think about things the same way I do.

To distract myself I do the breathing exercise, seeing how long I can go without breathing, each time a little longer.

I hold my breath until I almost suffocate, while looking at the hands of the clock. It's kind of like a videogame, except that you play it just with yourself. Each time, you try to beat the last time. The great thing is that you can do it at school and nobody notices.

Once when I was doing the breathing exercise Mrs. Squarzetti asked me, "What is the capital of France?" I looked at her with my eyes popping out of my head because I was about to explode, but I couldn't give up.

"Are you feeling all right?"

I beat the old record and shouted: "Paris!"

Spitting on my notebook, saying "Paris" as if it had lots of *P*s. There's still a mark where my spit dissolved the ink.

"Well done!" she said, terribly pleased with herself.

I know, I know, I thought.

I'd like to have a stopwatch so that I could time myself more accurately. I'd also like to be able to write with my left hand. I'm training myself to write with both hands like Leonardo da Vinci, who was a genius.

But the writing I do with my left hand looks like it's Blue's, or maybe the doctor's. If I write with it, you won't understand anything.

"Yeah, you're right. Absolutely nothing's going right today."

But can I go to the movies with Davide and his mother and his sister anyway? Today's Elisabetta's birthday. Can I? It's true that you can't go, but what about me, can I? Please let me go. It's an amazing movie, it could even help me with school. If I go, you won't be mad? And you're not just saying you won't get mad, but then you'll get mad anyway? Because I'm a little mad too, you know. I know it's not your fault. But I don't like to come home to this;

the apartment is too quiet when you don't talk. I can't talk to anyone. Maybe I could talk with Giulia. Do you think that's a good idea? That she'd understand? That she could help us? That we can trust her? That she knows how to keep a secret? That she'd be able to understand us? That if she understood us she'd find a solution? That there is a solution? That it will be over soon? That Giulia will call while she's on vacation? That you're worth something to her? That it's better if we sort things out on our own, like always? That we'll know how to sort things out? That we don't need anyone else? That I can do it? Do you think so?

Otherwise I could call the vet, who is a kind of doctor at least, but I don't know if that's a good idea.

I'm really not sure what to do. I'll end up doing nothing.

I could talk to a friend, but I don't know if I have such a friendly friend. Anyway, friends are crawling with parents. If they let anything slip out, I'm finished.

"It's all right, Mama, don't worry. Everything went fine at school as usual."

I head down the hall.

"Do you think it's my fault you died?"

I have to call Davide, to tell him about the movies.

"My mother said it's fine, she'll drop me off. What time?"

"At four."

"Okay, see you at your place."

Luckily I know where Davide lives. I'll have to take the tram there, but it's easy.

The people on the tram stink. It's always that way when it rains. Their coats smell like wet dogs. Or car seats when people have smoked there. Every once in a while adults stink. They've got bad breath, or hair that smells like un-made beds. Old people stink of old people. My grandpa stunk of really old people. He was really old. Grandma smells like violets and lilies of the valley, like napkins forgotten in a drawer. Mama was born by accident when Grandma thought she couldn't have any more kids be-cause she was already on pause.

"It was a miracle I was born, or a joke, you know? A joke of nature."

At the third stop I get off.

I arrive at Davide's house and ring the bell.

"My mother was in a hurry because she had to go to the doctor."

I go up.

Davide's house isn't bad. It's always a bit crazy. Better than Marco's house, where right away the maid makes you feel uncomfortable and everything is in its place, with the newspapers and books on the tables fanned out like in doctors' waiting rooms and you already feel sick, already sure they'll find something wrong with you: Hmmm, ex-actly as I suspected; try to cough a little. People who are perfect always make you feel like trash.

Davide's mother, on the other hand, always seems a bit disorganized. She wears long scarves and never goes to the hairdresser. She's always waving her arms around as if she's chasing away flies. She's agitated now too, so she's not worried about Mama not being able to come up. We have a Coke and then go to the movies to see *Ice Age*.

The movie isn't bad, it's just that all I can think about is what I'll do afterward; I have to make sure I get a lift without making them suspicious. During the intermis-sion, Davide tells me that tomorrow he's going to come to my place to do homework. This sends me into total panic, so after that I don't catch much of what happens to the prehistoric animals, and I couldn't care less if the dodo becomes extinct. For me a new age has come: We've entered the Late Liar era.

They always say that you shouldn't tell lies, but without lies I'd already be in an orphanage.

This, in any case, is my first true lie.

It's no use crossing my fingers or my toes or touching my nose for luck. I don't have any choice. It's just that in the movies at least you always have someone to face the tough times with. There's a main character in difficulty, and at a certain point someone appears to get him out of trouble. Maybe I shouldn't have come to the movies, but it was for the sake of the details: Someone who goes to the movies surely can't have a mother dead in her bed.

Luckily, when we leave, Davide's sister is wailing that she wants to go and eat hamburgers right away. She makes such a racket that no one wonders why I'm so quiet.

"Do you want to come with us?"

"No, I can't. My mother's waiting for me. Actually, she asked if you could give me a ride since she didn't know what time she'd be done at the doctor's."

"Do you want us to call her?"

"No, when she's at the doctor's she turns her phone off."

I feel like a genius. A genius who has just fallen from the eighth floor and landed without a scratch because they were moving mattresses below, like one of those crazy news stories that pop up in the papers every so often, when reality is stranger than fantasy.

"CHILD FALLS FROM WINDOW, LANDS ON GUIDE DOG,

Grandma loves that kind of thing.

Or else I'm like cats with their nine lives; they leap off the balcony to catch a pigeon and miraculously survive.

We get in their car and five minutes later we're in front of my building. Elisabetta says to me, "Too bad for you, you can't come eat with us."

I stick my tongue out at her.

Davide says, "See you tomorrow."

His mother: "Bye, dear."

And then she says some dirty word to a guy complaining because we're double-parked.

They wait for me to go in the front door. I don't turn to wave good-bye.

When I hear the car leaving, I think maybe I've gone too far. Someone goes to the movies and then comes home, and at home there's still Mama—dead in her bed.

It's not possible.

It doesn't make sense.

It's just a story I made up to frighten myself.

I like to read. I read without stumbling over the words, even when I have to read out loud, even when Grandma would make me get up on the chair and Mama would scold her.

"For heaven's sake, we're not at the circus."

I would stand there in my pajamas barefoot, like a parrot clutching his perch, and recite Manzoni—"He has passed. As stark and still"—and I really was still, until the end of the poem.

Words are wonderful because there are so many.

Best of all I like difficult words and long ones, like *antidisestablishmentarianism*.

Or funny ones, like *topsy-turvy*. There are lots of ways to talk about a huge confusion, but *topsy-turvy* is my favorite. So on the walls of the first-grade classrooms, along with the words *airplane* in the shape of an airplane and *banana* in the shape of a banana, they could hang a photo of me and Mama as *topsy* and *turvy*, the one where we look just like each other, like two peas in a pod, held together tight-tight in our shell.

Words are useful for working out what others are really saying, the ones who think you can't understand.

Words in a row make stories.

You put things in a row and make a story out of it. Stories put things in their places. Then you're more relaxed. The stories you invent are your personal lullabies. Even when they're horrible, they don't scare you anymore because you're the one who invented them.

That's what this is too.

This story is only a secret I told myself to see if I'm able to keep a really secret secret.

Now I open the door and smell meatballs in the hall.

Meatballs and mashed potatoes, my favorite, the meal Mama makes me when she has to ask me to forgive her for something big.

She's still there.

Usually she helps me do my homework. Or she checks it afterward. Or else she listens while I recite something in English. It seems like English is very important. English is useful for songs, and for PlayStation too. If you know English, you understand certain things better.

Tomorrow I have a test at school.

No matter what, I *have* to study.

I have to study, study, study.

If you don't study, friend, you're screwed. If you don't get at least a "Good" on this test you're in big trouble. They'll put a big black mark next to your name and call a parent meeting.

"Do you get it, friend? Dear Mama will have to go and talk to the assfaces who are talking about you behind your back. Who will you send, friend, the cat?"

"*Fucking shit.* Blue, let's get to work. Let's show those assfaces who we are."

"Careful, friend, if you use dirty words they'll fuck you up."

"Okay, okay," I say, and put on my tough-guy face. "We'll be the ones doing the fucking-up around here, friend."

No problem.

4

Something is different today.

Mama has gone hard and is swollen all over. Yesterday she was colder; today she's puffier. I touch the radiator to see if it's working—it's not. Mama's not working anymore either.

There's a layer of dust on the radiator. She hasn't noticed. Now it's all the same for her if things are dirty or clean, ugly or pretty, lukewarm, freezing, or just terrible. She's finished fighting with opposites.

My heart starts beating loudly. I can feel it in my belly and in my head, like a pinball racing wildly, smacking randomly into the walls of my body, elbowing me in the stomach, battering me with punches to the sides of my head, pounding my back, filling me with bruises and shivers. I can't stop it from doing whatever it wants, shooting all over the place.

Today I stopped hoping.

I look around and nothing seems like before.

I don't even know if there was a before.

I don't know if there will be an after.

I don't know anything about anything.

The blank notebook still covers my whole brain. This has to be how crazy people feel in their padded white cells, rocking from side to side, staring into the sum of all colors.

I'm rocking too, without even feeling like crying. I just feel like rocking back and forth on the edge of the bed.

"Mama's lost her spark, her mouth is oh so dark, no playing in the park..."

I don't know where the song comes from, I'm not the one who's thinking it. It's the song that's thinking me.

"Forget. Forgot. Forgotten."

"Forgive. Forgave. Forgiven."

We listen to the verbs being recited aloud and parrot them back. Then we have to complete sentences using the correct tense. My deskmate tries to copy me, but I'm in a daze, my pen in the air. I hear the sound of the words without understanding what they mean, like Ulysses with the Sirens, but to me they seem like police sirens.

"What's up with you? Are you daydreaming? What goes here?"

"Where?"

"Here! Third line, *forget* or *forgotten*?"

"It's the same thing."

No, it's not the same thing.

I don't want to end up in a home. *Forget,* I write, and elbow my deskmate. The torture is over. I stand up.

I hope I did well. I think I did.

I walk toward the front to hand in my notebook and it seems like I weigh a million tons. It's as if I'm made of concrete, with a stone heart inside. I feel as if I can only move like King Tut's mummy, completely stiff. I feel the floor give way, as if it can't support me, or maybe it's my knees that have suddenly gone mushy. I feel everything and nothing. But somehow I reach the finish line and force myself to smile. It's exactly like when you leave the dentist after having held your mouth wide open for two hours—it stays stuck like that and forgets how to move. My cheeks are sore.

"Very good."

It seems everything is going well.

The bell rings and we're free once more.

Davide wants to come to my apartment after lunch.

"Great," I say.

He says he'll bring *Snowboard*.

"Even better," I say.

I go back home. I plan my journey—carefully choosing the opposite side of the street from where the smelly flower woman sets up, so she won't get a chance to talk my ear off. I watch her across the street as she uses her poultry scissors to cut the stems of some lilies. She's got mean eyes and big, wrinkly hands. Until not too long ago she always used to give me a little pat when Mama and I stopped to buy flowers, little bunches of irises that smelled like bubble bath.

"Is this a gift, ma'am?"

"No, they're for me."

"Shall I put a bow on it?"

"No, thanks, that won't be necessary."

Every time the same questions and the same answers.

Mama tries not to pay attention to the old busybody. She drops a coin or her wallet on purpose, or she fixes her hair like it's no big deal and swallows a few times before saying good-bye. Then the flower woman's hand touches my forehead and it feels like there's the bottom of a shoe on my face or a bare foot with warty calluses.

I don't understand old people's obsession with touching children. They should keep at least as far away as the years separating us.

I walk past, as far away as possible.

But I could, I should, I would like to buy some flowers for Mama, because people bring flowers to the dead. People bring flowers to their lovers, to sick people, and to the dead (there's not a lot of common sense in all this).

Mama likes white irises or red roses.

"It may be a cliché, but if a man buys you red roses it still makes you happy."

I know what she means. I don't have to be a woman. It's that it's important to feel important to somebody.

People are ashamed of not feeling loved enough.

People always keep themselves to themselves. If someone thinks about you enough to send you roses, it means that he or she thinks about you a lot, that you're not alone. It's more or less the same with all presents. Actually, that's what presents are. That's why they matter even if they're not worth much. It's the thought that counts, they say; and about this, they're right.

Tomorrow I'll buy Mama some beautiful flowers, the most beautiful flowers of her life. But not today. I can't deal with the old witch and her questions and her sandpaper touch.

The last time Mama got flowers it made her very happy.

It was a bunch of red roses so big that it didn't fit through the door, and there was a little card attached with a pin. In her rush to read it Mama pricked her finger, then fell into a trance like Sleeping Beauty for a couple of days.

To be honest, she'd seemed happy for a while before then, strangely enough, and a bit absentminded. She bustled around in high heels, *tick tack tick tack,* and acted like someone who's just gotten away with something. That was a couple of years ago. The night before the roses she'd left me at home with the babysitter with the big boobs, Juana, and had stayed out late. I'd fallen asleep on the sofa between Juana's boobs, soft as a mattress, and Juana fell asleep too because it was past midnight.

When Juana heard the key turn in the lock, she was really embarrassed.

"Desculpe, senhora, but I've been up since six in the morning, so sorry."

Juana's boobs shook like Jell-O with a cherry on top, but Mama didn't even notice.

"It's nothing, dear, nothing to worry about. I'm the one who's late. It's my fault."

Mama seemed more concerned with looking at herself in the mirror above the chest of drawers than with us, as if some detail might have revealed why she was late. And in fact when Mama returned to the apartment she had a run in her tights on the right ankle; earlier, before leaving, she'd had one on her left. I'd tried to warn her.

"One should never arrive at an appointment with torn tights. If you have an accident and have to take your clothes off, who knows what they'll think of you."

But she'd been too busy getting ready to go out.

She apologized again, even gave the babysitter a tip,

and came to kiss me good night. Her perfume was different than usual, sharper. It smelled like the little green trees people hang in their cars.

It didn't last long.

After a few days the petals fell on the table and also on the floor. As Mama went down on all fours to pick them up among the chair legs, she declared that when the roses wilt quickly it means that it wasn't true love.

Whose love she meant, I never asked her.

In any case, that was one of the few times I ever saw her truly happy.

Or at least happy about red roses.

Maybe she's happy now too.

The light part of her has left her body and the heavy part has stayed in bed, like with a puppet. The puppets' stories exist even when they're sleeping. And even when people die, their stories still exist.

Once I had a high temperature and I thought it was chicken pox, because the next day I had itchy blisters everywhere. I was in bed but also out of bed.

I saw myself from the outside. I was moving around the room, obsessed with finding something, a bow and arrow, that should have been between the door and the wardrobe, along with a tennis racket. I had to hit an important target, that's what I needed it for, but I couldn't find it, and if I found it I couldn't manage to pick it up, because my body was still in bed. Only my will to pick up the bow was moving around the room, and my will had no hands to grab things with. It was separate from me, me who remained stretched out on the bed, mouthing words that made no sound or sense.

Mama says she needs lightness.

"But every day things are getting heavier. Even the mood at work is getting heavy."

Giulia raises her eyes to the heavens.

"What can you do? The fact is, they're assholes, every last one of them. Sure, if you hadn't ended up alone with Luca, you could have kept painting instead of working in that stupid office, but not with a kid on your back."

Mama makes a sign for her to keep her voice down.

"What's Luca got to do with it? If they're assholes, they're assholes."

But I understand, it's not easy to paint with someone on your back. Still, I thought, maybe if Mama stopped working and rested at least for a little while, things would get better. Maybe if she stopped working she'd go back to being an artist and paint something better than what we've got hanging in the living room.

Will there be any fruit juice left for when Davide comes over?

I'll tell him Mama's at work, but it'll seem strange if the fridge is empty and there's nothing for a snack. We need a little snack and some juice at least.

Supplies will run out sooner or later and Blue will end up with an empty bowl. Poor guy. It's amazing how such a small cat can eat so much.

The kitchen looks awful, like when you get home after being away for a while. I don't think Davide will mind. His house is always a mess, worse than it is here. Good thing at least there are some leftovers in the fridge.

I eat some gelato. Sometimes when Davide comes over he brings something. As long as it's not his sister's cookies, the ones shaped like hearts or stars that look great but then when you eat them you almost break a tooth.

I go and lock the door to Mama's room with Mama inside.

If Davide wants to go in there, I'll say that Mama doesn't want anyone to because I looked in her drawers. That's why her room is locked. It's not completely a lie, it's even half true, because I really did go looking in her drawers a few weeks ago. I wanted to read what she'd written the night before. She'd stayed up late writing in the living room and I wanted to know what was really on her mind. She'd seemed in a worse mood than usual.

I didn't find the pages. I found tights, underwear, and a red thing shaped like a willy hidden underneath her tights and underwear.

You push a button and the thing turns on and goes *vrrrrr*, like a blender.

Mama went through the roof.

"Never, ever touch my things again—never, ever."

Or your red thing, I thought, but I didn't say it, because she was mad enough already.

I didn't even tell her what I was looking for and why; it seemed impossible to straighten things out. I started to sweat like it was the middle of August.

"Have I ever come nosing around in your room? Have I ever opened your shitty private box where you keep all your junk? Have I ever spied on you?"

Who knows, I thought. I don't think so.

"Then why do you do it to me? What happened to all the respect I've taught you? Go on, tell me that!" Mama screamed like a madwoman.

"Don't use dirty words, Mama."

"Who? Me? Fuck you, and fuck everyone!"

Usually she doesn't yell, but that time she went for it.

She had a handkerchief in her hands, like the ones she keeps in the drawer on top of the red thing, and she was clutching it so tightly, it seemed like she might rip it to shreds at any moment, as if the whole world could crumble to pieces at any moment. For the first time I saw her veins climb up from her fists to her wrists, bluish and swollen. They were no longer my mother's hands but my grandmother's, or a man's, or a wicked witch's. Mama didn't seem like Mama anymore; she seemed like a really pissed-off stranger capable of anything.

The next morning she muttered, "Sorry."

I kept staring at my cup and the teddy bear–shaped crackers as I dipped them into the milk.

"Sorry, there was no reason to get so angry about it."

What a silly excuse, what a silly life, what a silly everything.

That time Mama managed to make me feel just like shit. Why she would keep a pretend willy in her underwear drawer is still a mystery.

A disgusting mystery.

I never thought of my mother as being like the women in dirty magazines. And I don't want to think about it.

Sometimes, in secret, Davide and I look at dirty magazines. His dad keeps them on top of a wardrobe, along with some movies too, because he thinks no one can get up there. On top of the magazines there's a suitcase, and on top of the suitcase a bag with pliers, wrenches, screwdrivers, and other men's things inside. Davide gives me a boost and I climb up because I'm lighter, and his fingers get red and swollen like sausages in the package.

My willy has much pinker skin than the ones in the pictures. Maybe they get darker as they grow, the opposite of hair.

It's not that I don't know that Mama likes to have sex once in a while. I'm sure that she did it with the last one, the one whose job seemed to be washing windshields at traffic lights.

"Vade retro Satana," she'd cry out in her little girl's voice.

"Vade retro!"

I'd hear her "Vaderetros" from behind the door when I went to pee during the night. Once in a while I'd also hear her laugh and I'd think, At least she's laughing. They have sex because, for some mysterious reason, they like each other. It doesn't have anything to do with that other stuff.

The fact is, now the room is closed, with Mama dead inside, and Davide mustn't notice anything.

When he arrives, he says there's a funny smell.

"I don't smell anything," I reply.

We play with Blue for a bit. Davide scratches him on the belly and Blue sticks his paws up in the air, like a dog.

"I told you a cat isn't so different from a dog."

"Why is Blue called Blue when he's gray?"

What a moronic question.

"Why are you called Davide when you're a moron?"

We end up in a fight.

"Stop it, you're hurting me! You're hurting me, ouch!"

I'm hitting him for real, not playing anymore. I'm on top of him and I'm holding him down with a strength I've never had before. He's shouting and slapping his hands down on the carpet like in judo.

"I surrender, I surrender."

I realize I don't want to let go. I apologize. "Sorry, I didn't mean to hurt you."

"What'd you do that for?"

It's never happened before. Davide is much bigger than me. It's better with *Snowboard*—he wins. I keep falling; I get the buttons confused; I can't get it right. I see the turn coming and can't help trying some fancy move, so I fly into the air and off the course, onto the roof of the chalet. The spectators laugh. Davide complains because he says playing like that is no fun. We drink fruit juice. And eat the last of the snacks.

"What do you say we do some homework?"

"Fine, I'll do it for you."

It's always like this; I do my homework and then I do his for him. It's because it's easier for me, I don't know why.

"You know, it's handy having a friend who's a nerd."

"If you don't like it, we can go back to fighting."

"Asshole."

"Whoever says so is a hundred times more than me."

"You want me to give you a Chinese burn?" He twists the skin on my wrist with both hands until I'm the one who yells.

Mama says it's because I was born at seven months, and seven-month babies are more intelligent. I was in an incubator for two months. Maybe I've fallen back in, because once again I find myself in an evil machine that creates horrible nightmares and I'm still too small to get out and move away on my own. I don't even know if it's true that seven-month babies are more gifted. In any case I only want to be normal.

Even if sometimes it's useful to understand things first.

At seven o'clock Davide's mother buzzes the apartment.

He thinks it's my mother, but I know that it's his. It has to be.

"He'll be right down," I say into the intercom. "C'mon, get a move on, move, hurry," I tell Davide, pushing him out the door.

Friday night. It's like taiga and tundra in the apartment.

Titicaca more or less everywhere.

I turn the key in the lock to Mama's room and peek in. I think about the door in *The Texas Chainsaw Massacre 2* and decide to leave it wide open.

Maybe there really is a funny smell. Maybe it's the toilet. Every so often it stinks because of the low pressure, Mama says.

Low pressure over the entire Mediterranean basin, but people don't seem to be any less stressed.

I turn on every light. In the freezer I find two fish sticks. I look at the expiration date—it's already passed. Doesn't matter. It wasn't that long ago. I put them in a pan with oil; I have to cook them for five minutes on each side.

I'm not even sure I'm hungry.

But I feel like I have to feed myself, so that I don't waste away, don't get sick, don't get taken away.

In orphanages the orphans always eat the same soup,

it's take it or leave it. I'd be happy to eat only fish sticks, chips, pizza, prosciutto, mashed potatoes, and meatballs. It's not really the same thing, though.

In orphanages you have to eat like all the other kids and with all the other kids, play with all the other kids, and sleep with all the other kids, even if you're not tired. From what I can tell, in orphanages you can never do anything different from other people.

I'm not used to that. I'm used to living with Mama, and our life is different.

You can be equal, normal, or different.

Equal is when you have to be like others. Normal is when you get to do great stuff everyone likes. Different is when you have a bit of a strange life that is definitely not equal, but neither is it normal; it's a life that's a bit lonely, a bit on its own, just like ours.

Normal is the best of all, but different is better than dead equal.

Equal is a bit like the sky when it's gray all over, like the bottom of a frying pan.

"Don't scratch it or you'll poison yourself."

Don't climb over the gate or you'll end up stuck like a chicken kebab. Don't climb over the barbed-wire fence or you'll get tetanus. Don't jump on the mattress or the whole thing will collapse. Don't stay out late or I'll be worried. Don't cross the street without looking. Don't eat like a caveman. Don't put your elbows on the table. Don't talk to people you don't know. Don't trust people—hey, what are you doing?

Nothing! Just frying some fish sticks!

At the smell of fish, Blue launches himself like a

surface-to-air missile onto the kitchen counter, knocking over the bottle of oil; he slips and slides like in cartoons, which makes me laugh out loud.

"It's not funny." He looks at me like he's really telling me off.

"Yeah, but it still really makes me laugh."

When the sky is like that, all gray and uncaring, with everything sliding right off its back, you don't think it can ever change. When it's sunny with a few clouds, that's normal. When it's stormy, it's bad but also beautiful.

With Mama, it's like always living in the moment before the storm: You don't know if it will come, but you know it could. Some nights you even hope it will, just so you don't have to be on guard the whole time.

Now the storm is here and we're all about to drown, but Blue and I are still bobbing along. Cats don't even like water. They don't let cats into orphanages.

I don't like having baths. But I have to have them because if I stink they might say: "It's a bit fishy when such a clean boy starts to smell."

When Blue fell into the bathtub, he looked as if he'd stuck one of his paws in an electric socket. Don't put your paws in the socket or you'll get electrocuted, don't stick your fingers in your nose, don't stick your nose in other people's business—he won't fall for it again.

"Believe me, a hot bath always does you good. You soak a bit and then you feel like new."

I turn on the bath taps and sit on the toilet. I check down there to see if any lichen and moss are growing—there aren't, but when I sniff my hand it smells like cheese. I pour bubble bath into the water, the one that makes lots of foam. I take off my clothes and realize that my feet have joined the Blackfoot Indian tribe. The mirror is all fogged up; with my finger I write *fucking shit* on it. I get into the bath. At first the water is hot, then it cools down. My willy floats up in the water, more like a sea anemone, those strange flowers you see in aquariums, than like the red thing Mama keeps hidden in her underwear drawer. I wonder if, as I grow up, it will become more like the red thing and make the same noise, or maybe just a faint hissing like it does now with the bath foam sizzling around it.

I've been in the bath long enough now that my fingers are wrinkled.

"Come on, get out of the water. Can't you see that your fingers are all wrinkly? How many times do I have to tell you?"

"I told you, dear, raising a boy is war." Grandma would stand ready with the towel with the blue and white anchors on it, a ham sandwich, and some apricots that had been in the sun so long they were almost rotten.

Grandma would always talk too loudly because she's a bit deaf, especially in the right ear, which is enormous and sawed in two by a dangly earring that's too heavy, and Mama would plead: "Please don't talk like that in front of the child."

I pull out the plug. When the water has finished going down, the drain burps, telling us that's that, I'm all done digesting: foam, pieces of skin, black bits from my feet, a little fart. I put on Mama's bathrobe like a boxer all in a daze at the end of the first round, and, since I'm here, I brush my teeth. Not all of them, though, just the front ones. In the mirror you can't see *fucking shit* anymore, just my face, and it's hard to read what was written there.

I make faces. I yawn, like a hippopotamus from the documentaries. I'm sleepy.

Where's my quilt with the baby-blue clouds?

First I have to go and say good night to Mama.

I don't really want to.

I'd prefer not to see her, and instead remember her more alive than dead, like with movie actors. When they die, the images we see are how they were when they were alive, not when they're all pale and wasted. That way you're happier to remember them.

The most they give us are pictures of the smashed-up cars, if they died in a car crash, like Princess Diana, who in my opinion was a lot less pretty than Mama.

The only picture I've got in my head of the famous vanishing Dad is of him and Mama smiling in front of a motorcycle, him with a red bandanna around his neck and her in a leather jacket, her long hair blown to one side by the wind. Behind them there's a house like a hotel, I think, though I wouldn't swear to it, because at a certain point Mama stopped showing me that picture.

"I lost it. I can't find it anymore."

So I stand at the door, leaning against the frame, dripping on the floor, unsure of whether to go in or not. I turn around and fall asleep on the sofa. I like sleeping on the sofa even if I have the painting with the yucky weather above my head. I'm a little scared about having nightmares again, but then I fall into a dreamless sleep, my koala on the pillow and Blue tucked up close.

5

It's Saturday, which is just as well.

School gets out early.

Mama says she doesn't understand why children have to go to school on Saturdays, when their parents aren't working. I don't see why that matters to her, seeing as how she never goes anywhere anyway.

"That has nothing to do with it. It's about sleep. At least on Saturday people can sleep in."

She's right, even if now it's not a problem anymore.

My problem is finding my shoes with the laces, because the ones I wore yesterday must sound like they have frogs in them. Everything is in the storage closet: Mama's fancy high heels that she hasn't worn in a while; riding boots, even though we only went horseback riding once; even swimming fins; but not what I'm looking for.

You pay attention to details and then go to school wearing swimming fins in the middle of winter. Not such a hot idea.

I put on yesterday's shoes, even though they're still

soaking wet. When I walk in them, they go *croak, croak,* or maybe it's more like the sound of Mama kneading pizza dough. When you walk in fresh snow, the noise is just like when you crack a meringue with a spoon. *Crunch crunch crunch.* When I was little, I thought snow was made by ghosts.

At least it's stopped raining today.

To make up for it, it's gotten colder.

I leave my pajamas on underneath my clothes because they keep me warm and because it's quicker that way. And anyway, at Saturday school nobody cares about anything because it's Saturday. Everyone lets things go, already thinking about something else.

Davide and his parents are going to the mountains because if it's rained this much here in the city, there'll be loads of snow in the mountains.

Chubby Broccolo's going to stay with his relatives in Puglia for one of their birthdays. They'll eat heaps of orecchiette with broccoli. I don't know what Antonella's doing, but she seems like the type who always knows what to do. The others . . . I have no idea.

Luca's spending the weekend at home with his mother, for all I know.

I've always hated it when they make you write about the weekend for your homework, or the topic is "What did you do on your vacation?" They do it to find out about your business and then use what they find out against you as soon as you mess up.

So I write a story about the adventures of Blue, who's a cat who seems like a cartoon. That way everyone has fun, including me.

Blue's ears are always cold, so I explain how when he

was made, after they'd given him whiskers, a tail, little heart-shaped pillows under his feet, and everything else, they realized they'd run out of ears. They had to attach ones they took straight from the freezer, but first they made a mistake and attached two orecchiette with broccoli, so he meowed in Pugliese like Chubby in the third row and no one understood what he was meowing about. Then they found the proper cat ears and solved the problem. We clink our glasses and say "Cheers!" to celebrate, and Chubby gets an "Excellent" on his homework.

Making it up as I go, and smiling, I get by.

Even better than poor Chubby Broccolo from Brindisi, actually.

One time before we had Blue I told a story about seeing a gigantic mosquito on the wall of the kitchen next to the refrigerator. It was huge, with such long skinny legs that it seemed harmless. But everyone was so worried about the malaria the immigrants were bringing into the city that they didn't bother with the details of my private life.

Our science teacher talked to us about third-world diseases.

"It's not the immigrants' fault if they bring diseases here, because it's not their fault if they're sick. It's because they're poor."

"Why do mosquitoes only sting poor people?"

"Maybe poor people are tastier?"

"Why?"

As we leave we all say good-bye. I wave ciao, ciao.

I've just gone through the main door when I hear Mrs. Squarzetti calling me back.

"Luca! Luca!"

Suddenly I'm terrified again. Where did I mess up?

"Sorry, Luca, but your mother forgot this the last time we saw each other. Would you be so kind as to give it to her?"

She hands me my progress report and gives me a smile, showing off a mouthful of crooked teeth, then turns—hurry-hurry—on her heel. It's Saturday for her too.

This is what the authorities have to say about Luca:

Luca displays self-confidence and a lively disposition. He is endowed with considerable intelligence and a sense of responsibility. The pupil succeeds in all subjects. He consistently applies himself, and the results are excellent. He has demonstrated a good deal of interest and ability in artistic activities and a notable interest in science and history. Kindhearted and generous, he does all he can for his classmates and is full of initiative.

The pupil Luca responds:

"Go fuck yourselves, every last one of you."

Assfaces. What do you know about being kindhearted, generous, and full of initiative? The only generous part of you is your asshole, the source of all your bullshit.

I don't know why, but I'm so furious.

Well, I know why, but that just makes me twice as furious. For the first time in days there's a blue streak in the sky that you can pick out between the raggedy clouds at the end of the street, but I don't even know what to make of it.

I march home with the report in my hand and the wind

in my face, with every step feeling more and more desperate to shut the door behind me—soon—sooner—soonest—as soon as soon can be.

The perfect image of a mama, the perfect image of a beautiful child, the perfect picture of health! Too bad Mama can't read it and Dad disappeared into smoke and I've got a fucking shit of a weekend ahead of me. Too bad that not long from now Mama's going to start to really stink.

Corpses stink after a bit, regardless of your sense of responsibility. It's a chemical process that can't be stopped. Even Lieutenant Columbo says so. After three days corpses stink, just like fish and houseguests, but getting rid of them is not so simple, even if you're bursting with initiative. I can't send Mama to a hotel or off to stink up some other relative's place.

You think someone's dead then and there, but it's not true.

If I tell you Mama's stone-dead in her bed, my artistic gifts will no longer be of interest to you; you'll send me straight to an orphanage to throw up little pasta tubes.

My eyes fill up with hot water again. Bullshit, I'm in the shitty bullshit.

And I have a whole weekend ahead of me.

It's strange. As I'm thinking all these things, I realize I'm already inside, leaning back against the apartment door to catch my breath, the little swinging cover over the spyhole winking at the elevator.

It's strange but I feel safer here inside the apartment, even with my dead mama's body in the bed, than out there.

It seems less serious. Here, inside, no one can hurt us. Here, inside, no one can pull me out just to put me in some other place I'll never get out of, where no one will care about me only because they're paid to care, which doesn't count. It's all a cheat. Like Grandma playing solitaire, when she chooses her cards and then boasts about always winning. I'm not falling for it. I try to turn the key again, but it's already turned as far as it can go. I sneeze hard two or three times.

Even if my hideout isn't much, even if here on the eighth floor it feels like we're living on stilts, like those shacks where all it takes is one strong gust of wind from the north to knock them down, it's still a home. Like the condemned building in the piazza out front, which has had a sign saying that since before we moved in, and nothing's changed. It's still there, and sometimes homeless guys sleep inside it. Since they don't usually have a roof over their heads, they make do with one that might fall in at any moment. I'm sure even homeless guys would say, Better here than in a homeless shelter.

I go to Mama and read her the progress report.

For the first time since she stopped getting up, I lie down next to her.

With my weight I pin down one of her arms under the covers.

I stretch out at her side as if we had all kinds of time ahead of us. An entire weekend. As if we had all the time in the world just to lie here side by side. As if my time were the same as hers. *Topsy-turvy*.

I know that she's probably not interested in other people's progress anymore, but then I'm not interested in her being dead either, in the strange blotches on her face, in how even with my stuffed-up nose I think I can tell she's started to smell. If everything weren't becoming so complicated, I'd say it's all the same to me, that in some ways I understand her, that I understand if she was sick of living.

It's just that maybe together we could have made it, if only she'd realized I was here, not just for changing the cat litter or growing up or causing problems. I should have told her that more often. And she could have made me understand more of what it was that really wasn't going right. We had a deal. I don't know if it was she or me who broke it.

Across from the bed there's a dresser and on top of the dresser there are pictures of us in silver frames: me in a swing; Grandma looking like the Madonna; Mama after graduating from college, and looking like she'd showed up at the wrong party; Blue, taken the day he came to live with us. Mama's dresser used to be Grandma's. We only put the nicest photos up there, with all the assfaces cut out because otherwise they'd spoil the scene.

I look at Mama and think, All in all she's a lot better than Davide's mama. Even now when she's so different.

I look on top of the dresser for the plastic bag with her makeup. It has to be there, even if she doesn't use it much.

I find lipstick and a tin shaped like a clamshell. I think it's face powder. Inside it's pink and cracked like a lump of desert, with a little sponge on top.

I go up close to Mama and try to put some lipstick on her. It's not easy to follow the outline of her lips; the red gets into the wrinkles around her puckered mouth and it smudges everywhere. I'm making a mess. I try to make it better with the sponge, adding some color to her swollen cheeks. I don't know if she's happy, but maybe she is.

She looks a little ridiculous, made-up like that.

"My beautiful celestial rose," Grandma used to say to her, as always saying everything and just the opposite.

I stretch out again and try to think about how it was before.

I close my eyes, trying to remember how it was when she had her makeup done properly and her hair combed, and her nice clothes on. Inside my eyes I can see the little silver rectangles of the photo frames. Inside the photos I can see her, elegant, dressed all in white, with baby me in her arms. I'm wrapped up in a blanket embroidered with little pink flowers...were they pink or blue? Pink, yes, they were definitely pink. Maybe Mama thought I'd be a girl?

"I told you, dear, raising a boy is war."

"Please don't talk like that in front of the child."

I suck on the soft, warm blanket, made for someone else, like it was her tit. I almost suffocate on a wool thread that gets in my throat, goes up my nose, puts down poisonous roots that intertwine with my veins. They grow and make me explode from inside, like the trees that break through the pavement. Once again I'm in the hospital; again the nurses steal my cookies. We're back at the beginning, like in the game of the goose we play at New Year's.

The goose that the flower woman ate for Christmas.

I wake up screaming. There's a dead body next to me! I scream louder. No one can hear me.

Everyone's away for the weekend.

"Upsy-daisy, up-up-upsy-daisy!"

Me again: teeny tiny, tossed up in the air, trapped in a girl's blanket, the chandelier with the crystal beads coming closer and closer; terrified they're not able to hold me tight enough. Please take pity on me, please put me down.

"Upsy-daisy, how wonderful it is to fly through the sky!"

I'm scared, so scared.

I scream. I scream like I'm in a horror movie; I scream as if all the bumps I've ever avoided, all the times I didn't fall, all the times I survived, happened all at once. I scream as if I were nothing but a scream.

The scream becomes hard like a stalagmite in the frozen cave of Mama's room.

I run out and swear I'll never go back in, never again.

I run into the bathroom to wash my face and hands.

Fear is all I feel. Again I have trouble breathing. I curl up on the armchair in the living room. I feel like I need to pee. I should get up and go back to the bathroom, but instead I stay huddled in the chair.

I don't want to cross the hall anymore. The hall is a Grand Canyon, a swamp infested with crocodiles pointlessly crying.

My reservoir of tears is dry again, but plenty of pee is leaking out. At first I try to hold it. Then I can't take it anymore. I feel hot liquid running down my legs, but at the same time I feel heat rising and rising through the rest of my body, so then I try to get the pee out more quickly. I squeeze and squeeze, wringing myself out like a dishcloth. The chair is stained all over. I know I shouldn't do it, but I like doing it. The circle of pee gets bigger on the yellow velvet, which goes all dark brown. I learn how great it is to piss like this.

Blue comes over. I blow in his face and he runs away.

I'm exhausted, but I'd like to piss some more.

From now on I want to piss everywhere, like a cat in heat. I'd like to be Blue and pee wherever I feel like it. I'd like to piss, piss, piss and never stop pissing. On door-frames, on chair legs, on tram seats next to old ladies with their shopping bags between their legs and celery stalks for their soup sticking out like surprise bursts of nature. I'd like to piss on my desk at school and hear the rain of piss drip down on the floor, *drip drip drip* like in some romantic poem. I'd like to piss on the heads of the parents, on the last line of the progress report, and blot out the comments from those people who can't judge me because they don't really know me, like when I spit out Paris with lots of *P*s on my notebook. I'd like to piss on the lives of strangers who think they know everything and don't know anything, and on my own life in which I will perhaps never see Paris.

I'm worn out.

I'd like to piss again.

But I can't.

I've got nothing left inside.

The pee reservoir is empty now too.

I'm full of emptiness.

It's only three in the afternoon.

Still in the chair, I look at the stain, which has gotten bigger and now looks like a blank map, like the ones where you've got to fill in the names of the countries, the cities, the mountains, and the lakes, but you can't do it because you can't figure out where in the world it is. My pants are warm and wet and sticking to my legs. I try to think of how everything will be when it's all over, even if it's just begun.

I don't know.

All I know is that I don't want to end up in an orphanage.

I want to stay in this apartment, which is beautiful

even if I don't like Grandma's furniture. I don't want to have a tiny metal wardrobe to put my stuff in and I don't want fluorescent lights that make everyone pale like they're in the morgue and I don't want to have to ask permission for every little thing and I don't want to drink raw eggs every morning like the nuns made me do and I don't want gray blankets and gray everything. I don't want to be afraid to stretch out my legs to the far end of the bed, don't want icy-cold sheets, don't want to be frozen with my armpits sweating cold sweat and penguin guano between my thighs because at the far end of the bed, at the very place where feet turn into stumps gnawed on by ghosts, there's the Antarctic. I don't want to slip down into the glaciers, where the cold bites your ankles. I want to stay here. I don't want to fall into the third fourth fifth world, all the way to the last page of the atlas. Into the third fourth last world where they sell children or their spare parts. At the edge of the world there's nothing but seals and penguins, and sea lions that eat their own pups.

And more than anything else, I don't want to live without my incredible cat, Blue. In orphanages they bring you cat for dinner, passing it off as stewed rabbit.

Blue jumps into my arms, as if he could read my thoughts, even though thinking about afterward, now, is very difficult. Right now there's nothing but a big now that grows and looks like a blank map.

At most, I can think about after afterward, which is much later in time. I can imagine how it will be when I'm a vet and taking care of cats that piss everywhere.

I can dream about getting engaged to Antonella, and about marrying her and making her belly grow with a baby inside.

About returning home and telling her how I treated an armadillo or a capybara, collectible card number 55, the one that's always missing.

About how I saved some very rare animals, including a sloth, the one that moves in slow motion like Mama, number 78.

About Antonella saying to me: *"Amore,* with those glasses you look like a bespectacled bear."

Because it's likely that when I grow up I'll wear glasses.

The kind that magnify details.

Some detail must have escaped me about Mama. Maybe there was something that should have made me understand that she wouldn't be waking up anymore. But even when I try hard to remember every detail, it seems as if she was the same as usual that night. Not worse than usual.

For dinner we'd had chicken thighs and potatoes, and she'd eaten them too. She'd taken two, leaving me the ones with the crispy skin. Blue had jumped up on the table and tried to snatch a piece of chicken with his paw, and Mama had said: "Don't give the bones to Blue, because little chicken bones can puncture a cat's stomach."

"Mama, why is Blue always hungry?"

She hadn't responded. She never does when I ask pointless questions. I just wanted to get a conversation started. I understand when now's not the time, but every once in a while I keep trying. If I play the fool a little bit, I say to myself, Maybe she'll have fun. If I make her laugh, maybe the sadness will go away.

The other night we must not have talked much because I remember the buzz of the refrigerator and the sound of the forks being laid down on the plates and the scrape,

scrape of her fingernail as she scratched off the label on the water bottle. But it's often like that, that Mama doesn't talk much. Mama's never been a chatterbox.

Actually, sometimes when she speaks she doesn't even finish her sentences, as if the words won't come to her, and I tell her, "Careful or flies will fly in," because she says it to me too if I sit there with my mouth open.

"Don't sit there with your mouth open. You look like an imbecile."

And it's not obvious that when someone is sad, it's a mistake to take medicine. Or that when someone is sad and it *is* a mistake to take medicine, the medicine will make that person never wake up again.

Mistakes happen.

Once I made a mistake, putting a bean up my nose while Mama was chopping vegetables for the minestrone. I did it a bit on purpose because I wanted to see how far up it could go, but I was also bored sitting there watching her being so focused on cooking, with no thought of paying any attention to me.

I realized I'd made a mistake because the bean wouldn't come down and I could only breathe out of half of my nose. Mama tried to help me, shaking her head with a look on her face that was half worried and half depressed.

"Do I really have to deal with a son like this, worse than his own..."

"My who?"

"Worse than everybody, worse than nobody, let's just drop it, so long as you don't get the idea to stick a bean up your nose again."

So after that I was more careful.

When I looked in her drawers, that was a mistake too.

But what does that even mean—every once in a while you can make a mistake and nobody should die.

This is all not right.

It's not right.

Not right not right not right.

The soaking-wet parts of my pants are all cold, like an ice pack you put on bruises. I drag myself to my room and pull out sweatpants. Before I put them on, I dry the dampness left between my legs with my dirty Power Rangers T-shirt.

I leave everything on the floor. Who's going to tell me to clean it up?

I'm the master of the house and Blue is top cat, my personal assistant.

"Assistant! To the remote controls! The master of the house wishes to watch TV."

"Remote controls ready."

"Ready, *sir*. You have to say *sir*."

"Ready, sir."

"Tail straight?"

"Completely straight!"

"Very well, Blue. It's good that you're here."

"Affirmative, sir."

"T-minus and counting: three, two, one!"

Blue and I dive into the cosmic universe. We float like heavenly bodies, him Blue and me celestial blue, in the stratosphere of the sofa.

"Blue, what are your antennae picking up?"

"Exploding white dwarf stars, sir."

"Like popcorn?"

"Yes, sir, very much like popcorn."

"Well done, Blue, I knew I could count on you. Initiate Mission Popcorn. Cross Hallway Galaxy, reach Planet Kitchen. Prepare to land, assistant, touch down!"

I set Blue down on the table and he seems more terrified than terra-firmaed. He doesn't like it so much when I make him fly through outer space, but he lets me do it, mostly because he hopes to get something to eat.

"Upsy-daisy, up-up-upsy-daisy! Not so great, eh, being at the mercy of human beings?"

There's still half a package of popcorn left. They're a bit squishy because it's rained so much.

Doesn't matter.

"Mission accomplished, assistant. Return immediately to the stratosphere."

Blue tries to run away, but I catch him. On the sofa again he purrs and spits popcorn everywhere.

Blue is an omnivore, like a bear. Sometimes he ruminates as if he had an omasum and abomasum, like sheep. Sometimes he squeaks like a squirrel. If you pay attention, a cat is many things besides a cat.

The day we got him, on my birthday, he looked like a mouse more than anything else. He was mangy and you could hold him in the palm of a hand.

The first few days he holed up under the bed. I shut myself up in the wardrobe out of spite. Mama shut herself up in herself.

Then Blue got used to us and we to him.

Soon it will be Mama's birthday.

Question: When people are dead, do they still have birthdays or do they stop?

Mama will be thirty-seven years old. I'll bring her a bunch of flowers—flowers are good whether you're alive or dead.

Mama is a Pisces. Like a fish, she lives on the other side of a sheet of glass that separates her from the rest of the world. Sometimes she makes an effort: She leaps from the other side and then she's a fish out of water. You can see right away that she's not comfortable.

"Horoscopes are all nonsense."

She always reads them, though, as if in her heart she really does hope to find something true in there: love, health, money, a new job.

"You're lucky to be a Gemini, the Twins, because Geminis are friendly and cheerful. Whereas Pisces have a melancholy nature and are a bit introverted."

In the movies, the spaceship floats in the sky, the astronauts are suspended upside down, and the stars trace horoscopes in reverse, like ours—mine and Mama's—where what happens is always the opposite of what's supposed to happen.

The astronauts move their mouths like fish. They speak, but it seems like they're mute because they're so far away that no one can hear them. They eat colored pills that they keep in the spaceship cabinet instead of in the bathroom cabinet.

Blue is still hungry. We're out of dry food and he ate the last can of wet food this morning. I really don't know what to give him to eat. I have to go out. Blue starts to chase my shoelaces, gets between my feet while I'm putting on my jacket, follows me all the way to the door.

"Wait for me here. I'll be right back. Don't worry."

I check the money in my pockets and find only five

twos, three ones, and four fifty-cent pieces. Like playing battleships.

How long can the money last?

In the little shop around the corner I buy a multi-pack of Prime Fillet cans and two bags of chips. I walk around the block to get a bit of air; I pass by the newsstand but don't stop. I don't have enough money for what's not useful.

When I open the door to our apartment, an unbelievable stench hits me right in the face. It must be Mama.

With a scarf over my mouth, I walk toward her room, and the stink becomes stronger. It's Mama who stinks—stinks to death like a corpse.

I drop the bag and, holding my breath, rush to the end of the hallway. I run to her window and try to turn the handle. It sticks, but with both hands I throw the window wide open and the curtains fly against my face like spirits trying to take me away. And I feel possessed as I turn around, trip over a shoe and almost fall, and reach the bedroom door. I feel like I'm going to explode. I close Mama and her horrible stink in her room and turn the key. I'm out of breath.

But now I have to run and open all the other windows too, all of them, as fast as I can. I feel like breathing so much, but I can't. Finally I fill my lungs with just the air from the balcony, letting in the cold that cuts the smell like a knife.

The stink stays stuck to me everywhere. I smell nothing but stink inside my nose, all the way down inside my belly. I sniff my hands—they stink. Everything stinks.

Blue circles around me, eyes wide.

"What's the matter? Why are you opening all these windows in the middle of winter? Why are you behaving so strangely? Why can't we all just curl up happily next to the heater?"

He tries to lick me, his way of kissing me, but I push him away.

It seems to me that he doesn't have his delicate stuffed-animal smell anymore, just an awful reek.

I see him and then I don't. The whole room is spinning around me. I hear a buzzing in my head, the refrigerator noise but louder, the noise of the red thing that Mama hides in her drawer but a thousand times louder. So, so loud and then, suddenly, not at all.

Maybe I passed out. I've never passed out before, but I imagine this is what it's like. Everything spins and you fall on the floor.

As if someone threw a heavy coat on top of you.

As if you were dead.

But you're not dead.

If I touch myself I feel it. I'm not sure how long I stayed on the floor, but I'm fairly sure I'm still alive.

Maybe I just fell asleep, like Blue does when you put the leash on him.

The coat, I remember, is missing its sleeves, but I can still breathe through the two stumps.

Or else I really am dead. Maybe that's how dead people feel, as if everything is the same as before except that they can no longer change anything. They see everything going wrong, but they can't do anything about it.

If I'm dead, sooner or later I'll start to smell like

Mama. It's so cold. The smell now seems less strong. The French doors are open, as if we were in the middle of summer.

I try to slap myself, but I don't know how hard to do it. It's not easy to slap yourself on your own.

"Take back what you said."

"No."

"Take it back right now."

"No, no, and for the last time, no."

Pow! The slap sticks to my cheek for a while, like a nasty hot stink. I spend the afternoon in the wardrobe, thinking I'll never, ever leave.

The stink.

I knew that it would come sooner or later, and maybe it was there before too, just not as strong. Or maybe it's because I went outside that it seems more disgusting, like when every day you grow a little and you don't realize it, but if someone you haven't seen for a while runs into you on the street, he says, "How you've grown!"

It's true, that's how it is. The things that grow slowly always seem the same if you see them every day; if you don't see them for a long time, they're different.

I never want to go into Mama's room again.

I hope the cold freezes her, like the mummy they found in the glacier. I search through my head to find something to compare this one with, but it's not there. I hope that no worms come, like they do with zombies.

Grandpa used to fish with worms.

"Just look at my lovable larvae," he would say, opening a plastic container, the kind used to keep leftovers in the refrigerator.

"You see these? These are the Kennedy maggots.

And these? Pope John. These other ones are my Marilyn maggots."

The worms of famous people who died in his day, that's how he classified them. The biggest ones got the most important names. He was very proud of his worms.

I don't want to think about worms.

I don't want to think about anything anymore.

I have to learn how not to think.

There must be a system.

If you don't want to listen, all you have to do is put your fingers in your ears and sing loudly. What can you do in order not to think?

My head is filled with ideas, stupid ones and not stupid ones; it does everything on its own. I can't control it. There's no switch to turn off the maggots moving in my head and then coming out my eyes, the brain with its wormy white spirals, like Grandpa's maggots moving in the cranial container that was hidden on a shelf in the storage closet instead of in the kitchen.

The TV stares at me with its giant shiny pupil like some Jurassic animal. I see my reflection in it. I'd like to be sucked through the screen to the other side, into the body of the television, like Alice going down the rabbit hole. Everything goes marvelously well for the kids inside the screen. Even if a story starts out with things being only so-so, it always has a happy ending: The adults make up, everyone's problems disappear, the dogs wag their tails and slobber all over the people's faces. It's true that the TV news only shows sad stories, but that's because the news takes the pictures from reality, things that really happened. Once they're sucked into the TV, though, they seem less real; that is, they seem real but fake at the same

marina mander

time. You're sorry, but not all that much, and mostly you just forget about it right away.

Why doesn't that work for me?

I never behaved that badly, and still I couldn't convince anyone to make things happen differently. Not even Mama took the trouble to live for me. Why?

What do the others have that I don't?

I'm now holed up under the quilt, just like in an earthquake on TV, even though the ceiling is still there and the walls are there and even the furniture, and the whole building is still standing. Even though everything is in its place: the sofa with me on top, the table shiny with wax, the chest of drawers with the mirror, the piss-stained armchair, the painting full of yucky weather signed by one of the cat's ancestors.

The apartment seems naked. I feel like I should whisper, like in a museum, even though I don't know whom to talk to.

If people saw me on TV like this, a pig in a blanket, I'm sure their hearts would break: "Poor kid," "What a beautiful child," "Look what's been done to him, my heart breaks just to see him." If instead they saw me in the flesh, alive and kicking and not decrepit at all, I'm sure they'd send me straight to an orphanage, as soon as they'd exhausted me with questions to work out how disturbed I am, because they'd never believe me. They'd never believe that someone would stay with his dead mother in the apartment because he doesn't want to go to an orphanage. It's too simple an explanation, so of course they'd have to look for other ones.

Saying that I don't want to abandon Blue would never be enough.

And yet sometimes the dogs that people abandon at highway rest stops travel miles and miles to return home. They show up at the door and say, Here I am.

Because dogs don't want to end up in kennels either.

Better to go back to their owners, even if they're bastards.

I don't know what I'll do.

But maybe I'll get an idea.

Nobody pays much attention to us anyway. Maybe that's how things will stay.

I go to pick up the shopping bag I left in the hallway. I put the cans of food away. I rinse Blue's bowl and put a little food inside. I cover the open can with foil and put it in the fridge.

At the same time I decide to start a new life.

You can't put groceries away and decide your future. You can't do two things at once.

And yet now I can; I can do everything.

So I decide to do the same things I did with Mama, just without her. It can't be impossible.

I tell myself: It's just as if you've grown up.

All of a sudden.

I'm your typical single guy and I'm stuck at home because it's very much winter outside. I just have to keep to myself. I have to make it work.

How many times have I wanted to grow up sooner, right away? Now here we go. It's happened. It could have happened better, but that's how it is. That's all.

What do single people do when they're home alone?

All I can do is imagine and copy.

I imagine that singles read the newspaper. Fine. That's what I'll do.

I pick up a magazine and read it. I like reading, why shouldn't I do it now? Mama's newspaper has an article that says that single people make up 25 percent of our country's population. Fine. Now there's one more.

I'm not an orphan. I'm single.

It's just a matter of words. Sometimes words can even change ideas and points of view. In order to be an adult, fuck, all you've got to do is use adult words. Like getting a driver's license: You've got to be a certain age to express yourself in a certain way—before, you can't. And yet there's no exam to test your ability to drive words in the right direction.

I can say all the dirty words I want, I can jump red lights now that I'm alone. I can also blaspheme, use the dirtiest dirty words of them all, because God hasn't woken up Mama and so he deserves it. I just have to make sure nobody hears me.

I have a go at God: *Fuck you, God.*

I have trouble at first, like when I have to stick out my tongue as far as I can to see if I've got spots on my tonsils, but then I manage.

It's not that fun, but I say it.

Fuck you, God; God, fuck you.

I could light up a cigarette too, if I wanted, and smoke it at the window looking out at the smoking chimneys on the rooftops, like Mama, who looks out and the smoke seems to come out of her head because her thoughts are burning up.

Mama's cigarettes are right here, on the table, and so is the lighter with the word *Love* on it, inviting me to become big right away.

I wonder if single people are happy to be single.

Whether they don't miss the good-night kiss and that face-cream smell that stays awhile on your cheek and on your pillow too, Mama's protective cream, which fights wrinkles and also bad dreams.

The good thing is that I don't have to eat tonight, or wash, or force myself to be cheerful, not tonight.

Tomorrow is Sunday, everyone's day off.

I wear myself out with comics. I've read almost all of them before. I crunch on cookies. There's a surprise in the package, a toy clown who runs in zigzags on just one wheel.

With cookie crumbs inside the quilt, on the sofa, between my teeth, I try to sleep. I dream about losing all my teeth, one by one. My teeth begin to wobble, then they slip out easily, without pain, without screams. The gums are left empty, like when you pull petals off daisies to play "She loves me, she loves me not." I don't know how I'll be able to go to school without teeth. I don't know what I'll do if I can't smile anymore.

6

Today's Sunday. No school.

It seems a lot like yesterday, and yet, school or no school, it's today. The sun is out, though. It's weak, but I can see it through a pane in the French door. I spot it curled up in the light blue clouds, with Blue beside me and my finger running over the sharp ridges of teeth that seem like mountain ranges inside my mouth.

Single people get up late on Sundays because they don't have anything to do, so I turn over and keep sleeping.

This time I dream about my friend Davide. We're riding bikes along a pier. Then a man shows up and says that bikes aren't allowed on the pier, so we pedal harder, because if we pedal fast enough, we might lift off. Davide breaks away from earth first and begins to flutter like a butterfly. His mama sees us from far away and moves her arms like she's swatting flies.

"Come here, come here before you hurt yourself. You'll burn if you stay out in the sun too long."

I pedal lots and lots but stay lower down. In my dream I dream of soaring up into the sky and turning in circles on my outstretched wings, with the seagulls, above all the houses and everything. I dream of seeing the sea look small like the sparkly piece of mirror that's the pond in a nativity scene, but I pedal like crazy and only seem like a bee, which moves superfast just to stay in place in the air. Then my legs can't take it anymore: I get a cramp in one of my calf muscles. I come close to falling; maybe I do fall. I fall but don't touch the bottom. I wake up first.

I wake up again with Blue asleep on my right leg, which has fallen asleep. If I touch it, it's like it's someone else's leg, as if they've put it in my bed in order to play another nasty trick on me.

I'd like to keep sleeping, but I'm not sleepy anymore.

I drag myself to the bathroom and sit down to pee like a girl. Mama says it's better that way because I don't leave drips on the seat, and to be honest it's also comfortable. I can stay on the toilet as long as I want, without even having to poop on command.

Today being Sunday, I'd like to celebrate and not take a poop and invent something new, but even if everything's new, nothing original comes to mind. The only wants that come to me are old ones, used a million times, worn out and faded by the tumble dryer of everything that's happened.

I would really like to go on a bike ride like I did when we used to visit Grandma, before she lost her marbles and they carried her off to Villa Serena.

"Mama, why don't we go to Grandma's anymore?"

"Because she's not doing so well."

Grandma lost her marbles—or, as we say, lost the *tramontana*—or maybe she gained it: the wind got into her brain and tangled up all her ideas.

"Does the wind do that?"

"Yes, sometimes the wind can drive people crazy."

The only things that come into my head are ideas so normal it's crazy not to be able to make them happen. But maybe I couldn't have even before, because Mama was tired and never wanted to do anything. For me nostalgia is only nostalgia for an idea, even if then nostalgia catches me in the stomach and it feels like hunger pains.

Mama likes to spend hours looking out the window, and it's clear that for her the outside is very far away. She's looking out the window of an airplane, not our apartment.

Not all that much has changed.

Sometimes, sure, if I really insist, Mama goes along with my ideas, but it's one thing to have someone doing things she doesn't want to do just to make you happy, and totally another if someone is *actually* having fun.

Now I'm a coat that's missing both sleeves.

When we'd go to the seaside to visit Grandma, who lived in a city with the sea right there, I could ride my bike every day. I'd swerve between the people in bathing suits who were in the street too. Then we'd stop to have a chocolate-and-pistachio gelato and sit in the sun, making fun of the chubby girls in the water with their life preservers made of chub around their bellies. We'd go back to Grandma's house at lunchtime, and when I stepped into the house it felt for a minute like I'd gone blind, because outside there was so much light and inside it was so dark. The first time, I was frightened and really thought I had gone blind, like one of those guys with the German shepherds and white walking sticks and pimply-looking letters they have to feel on the pages. I burst out crying, until little by little my eyes became used to the dark and I stopped crying and being afraid.

I also liked to lick the salt on my smooth tanned skin, like Blue when he grooms his fur. I liked the smell of the salt and the fact that by scratching the dry salt with my fingernail I could make doodles and tattoos on my skin like the ones Native American chiefs have. Then I'd have to take a shower, but I'd try to save at least an arm from washing so that I could lick it at night, under the heavy cotton sheets that smelled new even if they were the same ancient sheets from Grandma's dresser.

They'd say, "You're not a goat. Goats like salt."

Or:

"You're a goat, because you're ignorant."

But they didn't really think that. They just said it to make fun of me.

Cities by the sea are more beautiful because they're half town and half sea. I live in an all-city city, a *città tutto città*. That's what they call the street map: If you get lost, you can always check the all-city map, the *Tuttocittà,* even if you can't take your bike and go to the sea.

In the city we live in, everything is city.

I don't know what to do about this for now.

I'm forced to invent something else.

So I invent.

There's a rotting corpse in my apartment, so I teleport it to the emergency room. The forensics expert confirms that its anatomical-functional capacities are damaged beyond repair and says it's a fine mess. The vet, however, who's secretly in love with Mama, doesn't want to give up, so he asks himself if there's not something he can do for her. The vet consults with lots and lots of doctors from all over the world, and each one offers his or her own opinion about how to solve the problem. One says there are ghosts capable of bringing corpses back to life, that Mama can be reanimated if we find the right ghost or some good ectoplasm. In that case Mama could live with me, but only in the evenings and at night. Another says it's possible to resuscitate at least a part of Mama, the part where she's my mama and not just any person. Yet another says we could create an android mama, a kind of babysitter who's a bit stupid but who can do the job. A doctor from Egypt says we need to call a certain scientist who knows how to mammify mamas by wrapping them in bandages in such a way that mamas stay mamas even when they die, and wake up when it's really necessary. I tell him I'm trying to freeze Mama, to preserve her for as long as possible, while we wait for someone to invent some colored pills that, if you take lots and lots of them, will make you live instead of die. The vet says that's a good idea, that he'll start studying it, that we'll find a way.

Then the vet takes me out for pizza. Looking at me with his big eyes, made bigger by his glasses, he tells me I shouldn't worry, that he'll take care of it. On a Sunday the restaurant is full of people: There are couples, families, and us. I like that they see me with the vet and also the fact that he's a doctor—not that people know it, but it's easy to tell. He's nice to the waiters too, who are going crazy because it's Sunday and everyone is so hungry it's like they haven't eaten for a week. I try to cut my pizza with a knife and fork because I don't feel like eating it with my hands. I want to show him that I have good manners like he does. We talk a lot, not just about Mama, and it's not like meeting with the school doctors who want to dig into your business just to keep you under their thumb. He asks me about stuff like it really matters to him, and then he pretends what I tell him isn't a big deal. That's what he does when we take Blue to him too. I know Blue's not his cat, but he treats him the same as if he were his; that's what I like about him. We also talk about lions. The vet explains to me how it's the lionesses that go out hunting and bring back food for their cubs. He says that the hunt is successful one out of every seven attempts, that sometimes it's hard for them too, even though they're such strong animals. He also tells me about how one time a group of lionesses adopted a gazelle instead of eating it, and it was an incredible event because nobody had ever seen anything like it between such different species. Even the newspapers wrote about it. He tells me that, if I want, until they find the medicine to wake up Mama, he could adopt me, even though we belong to such different species. I'm happy because that way I won't end up in an orphanage, and Blue will have his own doctor all to himself. I imagine my new life with the vet who knows everything about animals. It seems so wonderful that I'm almost not sad anymore that Mama's frozen, and orphan-orphans seem just like poor creatures, a whole other category.

I'm wearing a white coat and standing next to him. I've got the sleeves rolled up because it's his coat. I'm helping him treat dogs and cats.

"Here we are, now hold him steady, carefully. Pet him softly and tell him how good he is. You'll see how he calms down."

And that's how it is. When the vet talks with the cats, the cats relax. The dogs accept the situation and become less scared.

At the end of office hours the patients go away wagging their tails, thanking us, and smiling. We wash our hands, swiping the soap from each other, and then we head to the laboratory to study; time passes and we don't even notice. We swap opinions like scientists do and pat each other on the back when we have a good idea. We're so smart, the smartest of them all. We'll figure it out for sure. Eventually we say good-bye to Mama, who is hibernating in a special capsule made all of silver behind a secret door in the laboratory, and we go home in Muddy Waters's Jeep, which is all dirty with mud from the savanna. When we open the door, Blue comes up and greets us.

"Hi, guys, how are you?"

Because the vet is so smart he's also managed to teach Blue our language.

I say to Blue now, "Hey, what do you think, Blue? Wouldn't that be great?"

Blue stays quiet.

I look him straight in the eye and he looks at me. His eyes are infinitely deep, like the Mariana Trench; nobody knows what's at the bottom.

Maybe Blue wouldn't like living with the vet. Maybe he hates him because the vet puts the thermometer up his butt instead of under his arm or in his mouth like with human beings. Mama says there's no point in fantasizing because there's nothing that's fantastic.

I eat potato chips, then I blow into the bag and burst it with a single blow, a gunshot. Blue is scared. He arches his back, leaps sideways, and runs away. For the first time in my life, I can't wait till it's Monday.

7

What an awful night.

As soon as I manage to fall asleep for real, Blue begins to meow like a madman. It sounds more like howls than meows, never ending, the meowing of an animal being tortured. I get up to see what's going on, terrified by the thought that Blue feels unwell too.

I always sleep with the lights on now. At my home it's always bright and always cold, like the North Pole.

I drag myself into the hallway. It's like my eyes are cloudy and my head's full of rain. I see Blue in front of the door to Mama's room. He wants to go in; he jumps up and bats the handle, jumps and meows, scratches the door, desperate at not being able to open it. I pick him up and carry him back to the sofa. He doesn't want to stay. I have to squeeze him so hard I can feel his birdlike skeleton under his skin. As soon as I stop holding him, he goes right back to the hallway. He starts to cry again and jump like a monkey, with a determination you find only in the most ridiculously stubborn cat.

I have to get up early, but I can't sleep at all, I'm

drowning in calm waters, flopping from one shore to the other. The covers are twisted up with my pajamas, trapping me.

I'm the one who tells the alarm it's time to get up this morning.

"And you thought you were the only one who knew how, huh, Assface?"

At breakfast I explain to Blue that Mama's room is *off limits*.

"Off limits, verboten, keine Gegestände, no trippen for catten."

It's just like the little signs on the windows in trains; there's no point complaining so much.

I'm in a bad way, my face swollen into a good-little-boy mask that could sag and fall away at any moment, like a decal that comes off in your fingers. I wash myself with both hands, letting the water slap me around. Back in my room I put on my pants, sitting this time, search for two matching socks in the drawer, and go through my sweaters. I put books and notebooks into my backpack and go over in my mind all the operations I have to carry out, like the pilot preparing for takeoff in the poster next to the window, the one with the tape all yellow and shriveled.

I put my second life on over my coat and set off on a special mission.

I'm Dr. Jekyll and Mr. Hyde, a werewolf, Spiderman or Superman, but my powers aren't so super. I don't scale walls. My fur hasn't grown yet. I don't transform into anything special. I dress up as a normal little boy, with combed hair and books that aren't dog-eared and all the details just right.

. . .

It's Monday morning and the stores are still asleep. The town is having trouble leaving the night behind too. All the shutters, like eyelids, are still lowered over the store windows. I walk slowly because I'm early, like old people who have insomnia and shuffle around at dawn trying to stay alive longer; like Grandma, who one day started talking to herself and reintroducing herself every time we saw each other.

"It's such a pleasure to meet you. I'm Ruggero's wife, and you're the captain's son, right?"

Grandma and her obsession with ships.

"Not just any ships, my dear, ocean liners."

"Yes, Grandma, I know, the ones where the brass gleams like in church."

"And where the polished floors are swept clean by evening gowns."

"Yup, those are the ones."

And always the same old enchanted cruise song.

"Who is this captain, Mama?"

"How should I know? Grandma's the one who invented all these stories. She's moved into an opera and shut out everything else."

Mama tells me to let it go, tapping her finger against her temple and trying not to be seen.

Even the flower woman's stall is shut up like an abandoned dog kennel. Maybe she's moved too. Or had an accident.

When adults arrive early somewhere, they stop at a café for an espresso. So I buy myself a piece of focaccia, a teeny-tiny one to save money. There's a half-eaten strawberry candy stuck to the coin, but luckily the lady behind

marina mander

120

the counter doesn't mind if the money is a bit sticky: "If only money would always stick to my fingers."

Along with the change, she gives me a free lollipop.

"How was your weekend?"

"Fine. You?"

I blah, blah, blah. My classmates' chattering bores me; they always say the same things. They're talking, but their voices seem to come from somewhere else, somewhere I used to live not too long ago myself. Now I've moved into an apartment one floor up, but I can't look down on them. I'd like to look the other way, but I mustn't, I must keep my head up and my tail straight. It's not so easy. It's like when you dream about being naked in the middle of a crowd of completely dressed people. You try to pretend it's nothing, but you know that you're naked, that you can't get dressed until the nightmare's over. I shiver in my coat.

In class the teacher asks us what differentiates *Homo sapiens* from his ancestors.

"The ability to lie," I want to say, but I'm careful not to.

I get lost imagining my ancestors who rack their brains about how to crack open a coconut, then the ones who learn how to use weapons like bows and arrows and become more and more intelligent. They walk around naked, but everyone is naked, so nobody cares. Then someone makes the first coat out of animal fur, and it's especially the lady *sapiens* who want it. They call it a fur coat and wear it when they go shopping. They buy shoes that make them wobble and that get stuck in the grating over the metro.

the first true lie

Mrs. Squarzetti *sapiens* must have gone shopping last weekend too, because today she's got new shoes, shiny and black like cockroaches. She doesn't know how to maneuver them so well yet, because after a few steps she turns around and sits down again at her desk. The cockroach-shoes appear and disappear from view. I feel like crushing them with my exercise book.

Sooner or later cockroaches will overrun the planet, advancing on mountains of leftovers with shields shaped like trash-can lids, because cockroaches are resistant to poisons. They don't die just because they ate a handful of bad medicine.

They're the most intelligent of all, even if it doesn't take them seven months to be born.

Chubby Broccolo has fallen asleep at his desk, as he always does on Mondays, having arrived on the sleeper train from Puglia that reaches the station at dawn. The teachers all know about it, so they don't yell at him much. After all, it's not his fault if he's got relatives who live so far away and he stinks like the train.

I'd like to sleep in a train berth myself. I'm also nodding off with sleep. I have relatives far away too.

When Mrs. Squarzetti starts walking between the desks like someone unsure of the ground beneath her feet, I stop gazing at a damp spot that reminds me of a polar bear, a potato chip, Lake Titicaca, and smile—the secret is to do well in all your subjects and smile. Smiling is one of the responsibilities of a good ant, who must do all he can to escape an endless number of plagues of Egypt.

We're all ants, even if grasshoppers are much cooler.

"Do you know what happened in the end?" I murmur to Davide.

"The end of what?"

"The story of the ant and the grasshopper."

"No, what?"

"The grasshopper that hadn't stored up any food for the winter, he ate the ant."

"That's not the way it goes!"

"Who cares, Davide, the story's much better this way."

I'm glad Davide is my friend.

the first true lie

8

I've run out of money.

Mama says money always runs out before you expect it to. That's true. I should have remembered and planned for it. I should have looked for the secret code for the cash machine, but I didn't. Now I've got to open that door one more time. The number must be in the document box in the bottom drawer. I don't want to, but I must.

One missed detail can ruin everything: a wrecked car in the river, a plastic bag caught in the rocks, a tramp's shoe, a motor scooter set on fire at the end of a match by supporters of the other team.

In the last few days I've stopped being so afraid, as if my second life had begun to rub out my first, like a sheet of tissue paper that makes everything underneath look less clear, as if my life from before is, bit by bit, becoming a childhood memory, a thought that buzzes in your head that you can chase away if you shake your arms.

Mama, on the other hand, is still in there.

I don't want to see her.

I don't want to smell the stink.

I don't have a choice.

I have to break the record for not breathing, I have to hold my breath with all the breath I have, hold it inside, suck myself in all the way to my asshole.

I must turn away. I must hold out. I mustn't look.

I clench my fists so tightly that my knuckles go white, like hard candy all stuck together in a bag, joining forces to hold out against the enemy attacks.

I have to buy groceries.

The supermarket is full of people.

I like overloaded carts, the kind you can hardly push around. That way, if you run into another cart, people say sorry, because with a cart so full, of course you have the right of way. I like to stop to inspect the shelves, and most of all I like to see if there's anything new hanging high above them. This usually isn't stuff to eat; it's all those things you can never find when you look for them at home: nail clippers, Scotch tape, wrapping paper, all types of plastic baggies, corkscrews, bandages, tweezers, cat toys, fluorescent bulbs. I'd like to be able to buy all the hanging things, just in case. Because you never know.

One time I came to the supermarket with Mama and she brought along the last trial dad, to pretend we were a normal family; it was a real pain in the ass.

"Can I get a new crocodile pencil sharpener?"

"What do you need it for?"

Same with the paper-clip holder and every bit of stationery I wanted.

"What'll you do with it?"

Same with a toy mouse, one of the ones where if you wind its tail it runs around in circles.

"Blue doesn't need any fake mice. He's already enough of a mouse himself, don't you think?"

As if he didn't know that not everything that's worth having is useful.

He wasn't interested in anything beautiful except Mama; not the towers of food wobbling in the carts, not the collectible family of prehistoric animals. I wondered if that guy had ever been useful for something himself, but probably not, because he fell into oblivion, a deep one, along with the pterodactyls and stegosauruses. One day he disappeared, and no one ever mentioned him again.

I can't take a cart now; I make do with a yellow basket. I get a box of dry food and cans of wet food for Blue; wafer bars, chips, mini-pizzas, milk, gelato, and bubble gum for me. I get in the line for people with baskets. It's a special line, different from the one for people with carts—we have less stuff.

Behind me is a man with a basket full of beer. That's all he needs, you can see it in his face. In front of me is a girl with tomatoes and mozzarella. She's superskinny, one of those girls who eat and then stick a finger down their throat so they don't get fat. Who knows what kind of pleasure she gets out of it. If you pay attention to details, if you look closely into other people's baskets, you understand all kinds of things. I realize I should have picked up a bottle of shampoo or detergent; anything that Mama buys would do. Even better would be a package of sanitary pads, because at the moment it's obvious that Mama's not around. I make up for it with some razors hanging up near the register. It's Dad who uses the razors, because I don't have a beard yet, even though I wouldn't mind having one. A beard is useless—you have one and then you have to shave it off every morning—but it's useful for dividing the men from the boys. It's a difference you wear on your face: If you have a beard, you can shop for groceries as you please. If you have a beard, there's less chance people will worry whether you're an orphan or whatever.

Luckily, at the supermarket everyone is busy and no one notices the contents of my basket.

When it's my turn, I try to act casual. The cashier smiles at me, so I smile back.

She has red hair and blue makeup around her eyes that sparkles under the fluorescent lights. Her name is Daniela; I know this because she has a name tag on her shirt. Daniela knows nothing about me, though, and continues to smile—she has a bit of green leaf between her teeth.

"It comes to twenty-two fifty. Do you have that?"

"Sure I do."

I put my things in a bag, check my change, and lose myself in the crowd. I slip between people carrying heavy bags. And then I'm outside.

Outside it's an afternoon like every other afternoon. Everyone seems slightly annoyed, as if they were doing things they didn't want to do, as if something fun was going on somewhere else and they wanted the pain-in-the-ass grocery shopping to be over with as soon as possible. They rush to fight for a parking space.

Only the Moroccans selling lighters on the street seem happy to be doing what they're doing. If someone stops to buy one, they rub their hands together. Or maybe it's not because they're happy but because they're cold, because they had to take their hands out of their pockets to make the sale. One of them wears half gloves, with his fingers half sticking out. He sticks out his middle finger and tells a woman wearing lots of jewelry to fuck off, then laughs.

He's got a gold tooth himself.

It's not raining anymore, but the cold nips the end of my nose.

Mama says that my nose looks like someone squashed a little pancake on my face. I try to lick it, but no matter how hard I try, my tongue never reaches it. It's too bad, Chubby Broccolo can do it, so I always lose the bet. It would be even cooler to have a long tongue like a chameleon's, and also to camouflage yourself like a chameleon so that no one could see you. You'd become a city gray and blend in with the building, become sidewalk gray and turn into the sidewalk, become sky gray and pray for it to do something beautiful, to open up and bring the good weather back. Opposite the supermarket is the video shop; I think about crossing the street to look in the window. They've got a cardboard cutout of Bruce Willis stuck up on the door, but it's like Bruce is leering at me, so forget it. Who knows, maybe he has a sixth sense too. After the video shop is the sporting-goods store. In the window they have real guns; you have to have a license to buy them.

I wouldn't kill an animal again. I did it when I was little and didn't know what I was doing. I did it to lizards, and even now I ask them to forgive me. Maybe everything that is happening to me is the revenge of a lizard that died for no reason, just because of a bad kid.

Then there's Intimate Secrets, an underwear store.

I wish my secret was small enough to hide under some underwear; instead I'm afraid it's so big you can see it everywhere, as if it was leaking out of my coat, out of my face and eyes, out of the grocery bag, like when you step on your scarf that's slipped off without your knowing and you fall to the ground, all because of a stupid scarf.

When someone looks at me, I automatically look down, like shy people do; they're always staring at the tips of their shoes. The only thing to do is go on, not to look people in the face unless they look at you first, in which case smile, remember to smile.

I walk extra fast. It's better to get back as soon as possible, even if I'd rather be going back to anywhere else, to someone else's life.

Everything seems far away. Swept away by the wind and the rain.

The other side of the street is unreachable too, even if all you have to do is cross at the stripes to get to the opposite side.

Crosswalks are also called zebra crossings. I'd love to ride a zebra and roam through the tall grass. The lions would lick my hands like Blue does when he licks cake crumbs off my fingers with his rough tongue.

I hope I don't meet anyone in the elevator, someone who might take a peek into my grocery bag.

Or a peek inside the apartment.

9

Today is Mama's birthday.

I know, not just because I have it memorized but also because I drew a circle with a red pen on the calendar with the famous paintings. To be honest, she was the one who drew the circle because I've never been able to reach so high, above the fridge, except with the chair.

"Don't climb on the chair because you'll fall. Don't scribble all over because then we can't read the dates. Leave it be, I'll do it."

On the kitchen door frame you can still see the notches where Mama marked how much I'd grown: two years, three years, six years... She always makes me stand against the same wall and act serious, while she puckers her lips in a stern, professional way.

"Keep your head straight. If you don't keep straight, there's no point."

But even if I try to keep straight or stand on my tiptoes, I still can't reach above the refrigerator.

The important dates—her birthday, mine, Blue's—are

all marked on the calendar with circles. It doesn't matter if things have changed, we should celebrate anyway.

I look for a birthday candle in the third drawer in the kitchen. I find ribbons from unwrapped presents, uncorked corks, unrolled rolls of string, and some Chinese chopsticks neither I nor Mama ever figured out how to use.

When we went to the Chinese restaurant, the Chinese waiters all looked alike and they all watched us and laughed at us behind our backs, covering their mouths with their hands. We kept dropping our bites of food back onto the plate or into the little bowl with the bitter black sauce that splashed everywhere, and they laughed like it was the funniest thing in the world. Mama shrugged her shoulders as if to say, Who cares?

"Don't worry about it. Try this spling loll, it's good."

And then the lice cloquettes, flied seaweed, steamed laviolis . . . That night Mama and I only used *L*'s instead of the *R*'s, blinging chopsticks back to our apaltment with us. We brought them home to practice in the face of the Chinese who laughed at us, even though I had a stomachache, maybe because of having too many shlimps.

I find the little sky-blue candles from last year, sink one into a wafer bar, and light it using the lighter with the word *Love* on it. Blue follows the whole operation intensely, mostly because the wafer wrapper sounds like dinner.

I put the wafer with the lit candle on a little saucer; it's not much of a cake, but it'll do.

We make our way in a procession, Blue and I, down the hallway.

Blue in his gray outfit and me in my most elegant pajamas stained with pasta sauce walk single file down the hallway, careful not to trip like always on the worn-out Persian rug that runs down the middle, which, before being in our apartment, was in Grandma's, where everyone tripped over it and swore at it too.

"Stupid rug, we've got to get rid of it one day."

We advance, as serious as can be, and stop in front of Mama's door with our special cake made of layers of wafer and vanilla cream.

I put the plate down on the floor.

The tiny candle lights the ceremony with a small, shaky glow that looks ready to go out at any moment. I'm small and shaky too. I'm not sure whether I should leave things as they are or blow it out for Mama, who's out of breath?

I decide to help out because the flame looks like the little lights that flicker in cemeteries and makes strange shadows on the walls. Or maybe it doesn't. Maybe it's just me who finds everything gloomy.

"Happy birthday."

I blow and in the same breath whisper "Happy birthday" again; even with all my practice holding my breath, it feels like I don't have much air in my lungs. I leave the gift there and walk backward, like shrimps do, so I can leave it without making a sound, without anyone noticing, a little at a time.

10

On Thursday my hair grows.

You can't stop hair growing; it's one more of those "inexorable processes" that scientists haven't yet figured out how to stop.

Hair grows at 0.00000001 miles per hour. I read it in *Strange but True*. I don't know how much a mile is, really; and all those zeros confuse me. Anyway, a little bit at a time, hair grows miles and miles, even if you've got plenty of other stuff on your mind.

Usually Mama takes me to the hairdresser before my bangs reach my eyes. She's a hairdresser for women, so I find it embarrassing to be there in the middle of all those women getting their highlights done. It's also embarrassing because the chairs are right by the window, and every so often someone passes by and sees me wearing a cape like Little Red Riding Hood's next to a madwoman with a plastic cap on her head and hair coming out of the holes while the hairdresser tugs on her goldilocks with a hooked needle.

Sometimes the Bride of Frankenstein turns to me

and says: "What a beautiful child. Do you like going to school?"

The word *school* makes me think of Antonella, and I sink lower in the chair just at the thought that she could pass by and see me in this getup. As if that weren't enough, then the other women butt in, staring at me the whole time like they've never seen a male of the species before. They're curious, they want to know everything, and they're looking for gossip, always reading magazines full of it.

I hope this torture will be over soon. I imagine that behind the jars of creams and sprays and dyes there's a magic potion that can make me disappear. Or at least make them disappear.

To be honest, Mama hates going to the hairdresser too, because then she has to make conversation, but she says it's necessary.

"One's hair should always be tidy."

Recently she hadn't been going much herself, but I still never managed to get out of it. It's another of those strange ideas adults have: If you're older and you've got a bit of a beard already, you can also wear your hair longer; if you don't have hair on your face, then your hair has to be tidy, like the moronic cut on the head of Assface, who in addition to having an assface also has a dickhead's hair.

I'd rather go to a men's barber, one of those that have calendars with pictures of women chained up and with tits as big as soccer balls bursting out of their black leather tops. I'd rather talk about the soccer match or the Grand Prix and listen to the men chatting, but Mama says she doesn't know any barbers.

"I don't want to take you to just anyone."

If I insist, she tells me to cut it out with the same old song and dance about a barber.

Now, in theory, I could do what I want.

The problem is that at school they think about it in the same way as Mama does; they would never believe that all of a sudden she decided to let me have my way. That's why I have to cut my bangs. If I raise my eyebrows, hair gets in my eyes, which is just as annoying as having a mosquito in your ear; if I pull on my bangs, they hang down almost to the end of my nose. I need to find the scissors and give myself a trim. I can't find anything better, so I try it with the nail clippers. The curly strands fall into the sink like hairy parentheses. I thin things out here and there like the hairdresser does, more or less. It's a job well done, I'd say.

the first true lie

11

Mrs. Squarzetti tells us the story of a box that has all the evils of the world inside. If you open it, they all get out.

When she passes between the rows of desks, she fluffs my hair.

She's never done that before.

I'm bored. It's a sneaky kind of boredom, with an after-taste of orange jam, the kind that seems sweet but then has bitter peels inside.

The box with Mama's documents, the one where she kept her secret code for the bank machine, is still on the sofa.

Sometimes Mama asks:

"Will you bring me the box with the papers?"

It's a shoe box with one side slightly crushed in, held shut with an old rubber band.

I want to open it and I don't want to open it, like when you're at the movies and you put your hands over your eyes at a scary part, but then you spread your fingers to peek anyway. I found the secret code for the cash machine, but I didn't search for anything else.

Now I wonder if the box might hold some other secret. I find old bills, letters from the bank, a paper clip that gets under my nail and stabs me, pages full of figures in columns, but nothing to figure out, not even a reason why. Maybe that's hidden somewhere else.

Sucking my finger, I wonder where.

There's a little picture of Mama copied four times in a square, one of those taken in a booth at the train station and then stuck onto documents. The picture didn't come out so well because it's in black and white and because Mama's missing a piece of her head; it's hard to adjust the stool to the right height.

Davide and I also had our picture taken together last year and our heads ended up half outside the frame, in our case from the nose down.

I take it anyway and before falling asleep I put it under my pillow, next to a Madonna album cover. I always put something under my pillow. Usually I choose the things I'd like to dream about.

This time I put Mama times four.

12

Nearly two weeks have gone by and everything just carries on automatically.

I'm having T-shirt problems—I've run out of clean ones—and all my socks are dirty and I can't change underwear every morning anymore. I rotate them, though, so they last longer. They're underclothes, after all—no one can see if they're dirty or clean.

I should use the washing machine, but I don't know how it works. The dresser drawers look like there's been an earthquake in there, but to avoid worrying about it, all I have to do is close them. My coat is full of cat hair.

The other night I even tried to smoke one of Mama's cigarettes, just to see how satisfying they really are, if it's true they soothe anxiety and make people less nervous. It was like saying *Fuck you, God,* nothing special, aside from the bitter taste it left in my mouth.

The apartment, at any rate, seems not to have noticed anything.

Except for the table in the living room: There's dust on one side and shiny wood on the other, where Blue usually lies down. If dust has been piling up for days, he uses his tail like a feather duster.

As far as everything else goes, there's no big difference.

Every so often I feel like crying, but I don't know anymore if I'm crying for me or for Mama. I cry when I think about how I can't go into her room anymore like I used to when I couldn't sleep. I'd go to her and plead:

"C'mon, can I stay in here for a while?"

And she'd say to me:

"Okay, but just this once. You're a big boy now who should sleep in his own room."

Now that I never, ever want to open her door at the end of the hallway, I feel like crying. I don't know why—if it's for me who's shut out or for her who's shut in.

I need a place to rest; I'm so tired all the time. I don't feel like doing anything, just like when I'm recovering from a cold. Sometimes I fall asleep with my head on Blue's belly. I listen to his breath going in and out. I like hearing his heartbeat despite everything.

It's really cold in the apartment, but the cold freezes the stink.

Blue launches sneeze attacks, but it's no big deal, cats come with their very own little fur coats. I've stopped taking off my clothes. Before going to bed I take a fizzy aspirin. I hold the glass close to my ear because as the aspirin dissolves it makes the sound the sea does when the foamy waves sizzle on the rocks.

Once a day I'm frightened, because I hear the alarm clock on Mama's bedside table go off. Every day the alarm alarms me, as if I've never heard it before. Then I remember everything. Then I slam my head down—left, right—to get rid of the thought.

• • •

When I see Antonella coming over to me during recess, I think I'm dreaming. It can't be true that she's looking at me; she's never looked at me before. When she looks toward me, what she's actually doing is looking through me. Her gaze is an astral sword that stabs without wounding, as if I were transparent, made of special invisible ink that she can't read. Or doesn't want to.

And yet Antonella is coming over to me. And she appears to be smiling.

"Ciao, Luca, I wanted to give you this."

Antonella hands me an orange card, orange like the sunset on a school notebook, the sunset with palm trees on a poster for the Maldives.

"What is it?"

It's the first time the two of us have ever talked face-to-face alone.

It's the first time I can count the freckles on her nose, cinnamon sprinkles on whipped cream.

I say, "What is it?"

I can't think of anything better to say.

"It's for my Carnevale party. You have to come in costume."

"Oh, great, thanks."

"Yeah, it'll be so much fun!"

Now, when you're playing a videogame, it can happen that you don't know what to do. There's a fifty percent chance. Sometimes things work out, sometimes they don't. The important thing is to choose; otherwise the game can't go on. And now I can't choose. Or it's more that I have to choose not to play. No costume party, no freckle confetti on fresh snow, no Antonella, no nothing.

"I can't come, sorry."

"Why?"

"I'm going on a ski vacation that week."

"Why didn't you say so before?"

"I forgot about it."

"Why don't you do the ski vacation the week after?"

"Because the week after there'll be no more snow."

"Wow, you should be a weatherman! How do you know?"

"What do you care?"

"I knew you were kind of an asshole anyway. I only invited you because you're an orphan."

There were lots of people on the beach, all happy to be on vacation: waiters carrying trays of cold drinks with little umbrellas in them; big umbrellas protecting the tourists from the sun; kids in the kids' pool; and palm trees like in the Maldives where Antonella goes on vacation, where Antonella celebrates her Carnevale, where Antonella does what she wants. And then a wave rose up, but nobody noticed: The kids kept splashing in the kids' pool, holding on to little swan or crocodile life preservers; the mothers protected themselves from the sun; and only someone lifting a hand to his forehead, like a soldier does to peer at the enemy, saw the horizon and the sea behaving so strangely. Then the wave came and everybody died. An angry wave that wiped out everything.

All I say to Antonella is:

"I'm sorry."

She doesn't hear me; she's already gone back to class.

I don't say anything else.

I stand there imagining the news reports of disaster after disaster, all featuring me, following one after another in my head.

I keep my mouth shut until class is over for the day and I keep it shut as I walk away. I get home, still as silent as a mouse, and enter the lobby, then go up in the elevator. My anger, mixing with saliva, rises from floor to floor, flaring up inside me with every beep of the floor buttons, an enormous, deafening anger impossible to peer at from far away, a silent anger powerful enough to wipe out everything.

I lay my anger down on the sofa, beside my backpack full of un-dog-eared books and my blank, wordless notebook.

"Wait for me here. You too, Blue, wait just a little longer. I have to go to the bathroom."

With my head in the toilet of my mini-adult's life, forced to wear masks every day, Carnevale or not, I vomit up a slimy white soul, like snot or the stuff I saw squirted on some whore's tits in one of Davide's dad's porno movies, a stringy soul that looks like slobber, that tastes as bitter as bile, and that sticks to the bowl and to my chin, making snail trails that ping back and then freeze because it's so cold, streamers of pure grossness. Hugging the toilet bowl, I become big and liquid like a fucking shit.

Mama said she suffered from loneliness, that loneliness was like a whistling in her ear, like ships that set sail long ago, and she'd never reach them, not even if she swam.

Mama said that once all the ships and trains have departed, there's nothing left to do.

She said that's how she felt, on the shore, in the empty station, having arrived to life too late.

I can hear a whistling in my ear too.

But it's not a whistle.

It's the doorbell.

It rings and rings and won't stop ringing. Maybe somebody's stuck some chewing gum on it as a joke.

I don't know why, but I get up from the toilet bowl and go to open the door.

the first true lie

About the Author

Marina Mander is the author of *Manuale di ipocondria fantastica* (A fantastical manual of hypochondria, 2000), *Catalogo degli addii* (A catalogue of good-byes, 2010), and *Nessundorma* (Nobody is sleeping, 2013). This is her first U.S. publication. She lives in Milan and works in publishing.

About the Translator

Stephen Twilley is managing editor of the online review *Public Books* and the translator of several books from the Italian, including Francesco Pacifico's *The Story of My Purity* and Fabio Stassi's *Charlie Chaplin's Last Dance*.

31901055277919